Kendra Kandlestar and the
Box of Whispers

This book belongs to

Kendra Kandlestar and the Box of

Whispers

Written and Illustrated
by Lee Edward Födi

Brown Books 🅱🅱 Dallas, Texas

For information, please contact:

Brown Books Publishing Group
16200 North Dallas Parkway, Suite 170
Dallas, Texas 75248
www.brownbooks.com
972-381-0009

ISBN: 1-933285-10-9 (Hardbound)
ISBN: 1-933285-11-7 (Paperback)
LCCN: 2005906371

Also written & illustrated by Lee Edward Födi:

Corranda's Crown

Find out more about Lee Edward Födi at www.leefodi.com

for **Gabriella**,
and all those who are
wont to peer inside their
own whispering
boxes . . .

LIST OF CHAPTERS

CHAPTER 1

A Dark Shadow

It is entirely possible that you have heard stories like this one before. You know the type: tales of high adventure, where you read about little folk with brave hearts seeking some magic treasure in lands treacherous and unknown. Where danger lurks around every crook and bend in the trail. Where creatures more fierce than your darkest nightmare prowl amidst even darker shadows. And where, they say, sometimes heroes are born.

Well, in that regard, this tale is no different. But what does set this story apart is one tiny frightening thing. I suppose it's a thing that might not seem frightening at all to you at first. At least not as terrifying as some of the things in those other stories, like an ancient hag, hunchbacked and cackling with three crooked fangs, or a goblin with scaly gray skin and one yellow eye that glints like a bright gold coin in a dungeon's dim corner. No, this tiny thing doesn't seem dangerous at all compared to the fiendish villains in those other stories.

And now you wonder what this thing can be. Can you guess? No? Then let me tell you.

It is, believe it or not, a secret.

A secret, you say? How can a secret be frightening? Well, we will certainly come to that. But not quite yet. First, we must go to the beginning of the story. To get to the beginning, we must go to the land of Een during a time long ago when the world still remembered some of its magic. These were the days when ancient races, such as Dwarves and Elves, still roamed the earth. But even then, the land of Een was not an easy place to find. It was tucked in between the cracks of here and there, a tiny, quiet place that the sharpest eye would miss.

Here, at the beginning of our story, a young Een girl was staring up with a frown at a row of unusually large carrots. The girl's name was Kendra Kandlestar, and she was eleven years old. As for the carrots, they were unusually large because they were magic, or more accurately stated, Kendra had used magic to plant them. In fact, she had only planted them that very morning, and by noon, they had grown taller than the garden shed—with no end in sight. Kendra sighed. It had seemed like a marvelous idea at the time. Now that the carrots were looming over her like so many orange towers, well, she wasn't so sure.

She tugged on her long braids and furled her brow, deep in thought. Tugging helped her think. Thankfully, she had many braids. Her hair was long and brown, the perfect type for braiding. She had seven braids in all, reaching out from her small head like the rays of a star. Of course, Eens are known for their braiding ability, though I suppose if you have heard of Eens at all, perhaps it's not their braids that you will recall. Most likely, what you may have heard—and if you have not, I will tell you now—is that the Eens are a tiny sort of people, smaller than rabbits but bigger than mice. They are also a very old people, which is to say they have been in the world for a long time, longer than most. Some scholars and other such people who study these things think Eens are related to Gnomes or Elves. But this is mostly because Eens have pointed ears and seem to know a thing or two about magic. They can talk to animals the same as you and I can talk to each other, and indeed, many an Een town is populated with all sorts of forest critters. These are mostly the small, friendly type of critters, the ones that aren't about to go eating Eens for lunch.

Eens come in many shapes and sizes, though it is safe to say that they are mostly small, mostly friendly, and—most of all—afraid of the big outside that exists beyond the magic curtain. This magic curtain is like a giant invisible wall that separates and hides the land of Een from the rest of the known world. But we shouldn't blame the Eens for being so timid. In the world that exists beyond the magic curtain lurk all sorts of dangerous monsters, including Ungers, Krakes, and Goojuns (both the lesser and greater varieties, if you happen to know or care that there is more than one type of Goojun at all). Of course, if you were as tiny as an Een, then you would know that the world is a hard enough place in which to live, never mind Ungers and Goojuns and such. To an Een, a flower might as well be a tree, or a rock might as well be a mountain.

Of course, Kendra's carrots were another matter altogether. They would have been considered enormous even in our world.

"Uncle Griffinskitch is going to have a perfect fit when he comes home," Kendra declared, tugging on her braids extra hard.

Then, as if he had been waiting for his name to be mentioned, Uncle Griffinskitch appeared, stepping out from behind one of the giant carrots.

"Kendra!" the old Een bellowed. His voice was deep and loud, though to a person the size of you or me, it would have seemed scarcely louder than a whisper. "What have you done now?"

With a gulp, Kendra turned to face her uncle. "Th-th-the carrots have grown out of control," she stammered.

"Humph," Uncle Griffinskitch muttered.

Uncle Griffinskitch said "humph" a lot, though Kendra had long ago learned that humph didn't always mean the same thing. For example, a quiet humph meant that her uncle was deep in thought, while a louder humph, the sort that came from the bottom of the old Een's throat, meant that he was more than just a little angry. Then there was the roaring sort of humph that meant . . . well, it usually meant that Kendra had really done it this time. Of course, as long as he was in the humph stage, Kendra knew she was only in a tiny bit of trouble. It was when Uncle Griffinskitch yelled, "Days of Een!" that it meant extra chores for a week. Kendra wasn't sure what "Days of Een" meant. No one else she knew ever said it, though she did find the phrase once in an old book in her uncle's study. It began, "In the Days of Een, when all were one . . ." But that's all she could remember because it had been a long time ago when she read it.

Uncle Griffinskitch glared hard at Kendra with his sharp blue eyes. "Someone," he said, "has been playing with magic."

Magic, of course, was something Uncle Griffinskitch knew about. He was a wizard, after all, and a powerful one at that. It was one of the reasons he sat on the Council of Elders. Kendra liked to think that another reason was his beard, for it was so long and white that she could not help but to think of elders when she looked at it. Some Eens claimed that Uncle Griffinskitch had never once trimmed his beard or long whiskers. Kendra didn't know about that, but she was pretty sure the beard slowed her uncle down. He never seemed to move faster than the pace of a snail going uphill, despite the help of the short wooden staff that he always clutched in his withered old hands.

"I thought a little magic might help the carrots grow,"

Kendra told her uncle sheepishly.

"Humph," Uncle Griffinskitch muttered as he eyed a large book lying in the grass near Kendra's feet. "What's this? *Gardening with Magic.* How many times have I told you to not borrow my books without asking?"

"Yes, but I thought I could surprise you—," Kendra began.

"I'm surprised all right," Uncle Griffinskitch interrupted. "Unfortunately, it is a surprise of the unpleasant variety."

"Er . . . can we stop them from growing?" Kendra asked.

"What's that?" Uncle Griffinskitch muttered, stroking his beard and gazing intently upon the carrots. "Yes, of course. A Goojun's sneeze would do it."

"A Goojun sneeze!" Kendra cried, tugging on her braids. "How would we get one? From one of their handkerchiefs?"

"Goojuns aren't exactly the sort to use handkerchiefs," Uncle Griffinskitch snorted.

"Oh," Kendra said. "So what then? I thought it was forbidden to go near Goojuns."

"Humph," Uncle Griffinskitch said. "It's not forbidden to go near them. Just to help them. Them and any other monster that lives out there."

He pointed a crooked finger into the distance, towards the magic curtain and the world that lay beyond. Kendra followed his gesture to the horizon, but she could see nothing except the vast blue sky. Of course, this was no surprise. No one could see the magic curtain, not even Uncle Griffinskitch, for it was completely invisible to the naked eye.

Kendra was just about to look away when suddenly she did see something in the sky. It was just a dot, far in the distance, and it made Kendra gulp. She had seen dots in the sky before, of course. They usually just turned out to be birds. But what made Kendra take particular notice of this dot was that it was quickly becoming more than a dot. With every second, it was becoming larger and larger, plowing through the clouds like a giant cloak of darkness—and it was heading straight their way!

"What is that thing?" Kendra cried.

Uncle Griffinskitch couldn't even muster a humph, and if he had, Kendra wouldn't have heard it anyway. For now, a shriek came from the dark shadow, so loud and piercing that the world seemed to come to a sudden stop. If you had heard the shriek, you might have said that it sounded like long fingernails scratching a chalkboard. Or that it was like the blood-curdling cry of a baboon, deep in the wilds of Africa. Or maybe you might have said that it sounded like the screech of a skidding car, the type of sound that sends a shiver down your spine and frightens you to your very toes.

This shriek was worse than all of those sounds mixed together. It was so loud that Kendra had to put her hands to her ears just to try to block out the tiniest bit of the bone-jarring howl. It was the type of sound you could feel, the type that had weight. Indeed, it was so heavy that one of the giant carrots even cracked and smashed to the earth in a brilliant burst of orange.

The shadow itself was as large as the shriek was loud, casting a darkness so wide and gloomy that it seemed as if night had suddenly fallen. Kendra and Uncle Griffinskitch craned their necks as the ominous shape tore through the plants and trees above them, but all was black. Then, in a flash, both the shadow and the sound were gone. The silence was blissful, but it only lasted for a second. In what seemed like one beat of a tiny Een heart, the shadow returned, zooming back with an even louder, more triumphant roar.

Then, just like that, it disappeared all together.

"Days of Een!" Uncle Griffinskitch cried after a few moments. His sharp blue eyes, framed with wrinkles, were still locked on the now-empty sky, and his whole body was trembling.

"What was that thing?" Kendra asked.

"Humph," the old wizard muttered, and it was the kind of humph that Kendra had never heard from her uncle's lips. It was the kind of humph that suggested grave trouble.

"Hurry," Uncle Griffinskitch said, casting a worried glance at Kendra. "We must go at once to the Elder Stone!"

CHAPTER 2

The Strange Inventions of Ratchet Ringtail

Uncle Griffinskitch now moved at a pace that would definitely leave all snails behind, downhill, up-hill—or any hill. Kendra had never seen her uncle go with such quickness, and for once, she was the one who had to keep up.

She had only been keep-ing up for a very short time when a small gray mouse came darting around a cor-ner in the path, running so fast that he blundered right into Uncle Griffinskitch. The old wizard was sent to the ground in an explosion of white hair.

"Humph! Who's in such a hurry that he can't mind where he's going?" Uncle Griffinskitch grumbled, pulling himself up from the dust.

"Why, it's Oki!" Kendra exclaimed.

Oki was not only Kendra's best friend but also an after-school messenger for the elders of Een. The mouse was very excitable by nature and was now panting so hard that he could barely speak.

"I'm sorry, Elder Griffinskitch," Oki squeaked. "I didn't mean to bump you! But I was just on my way to find you. Something terrible has happened!"

"I know," Uncle Griffinskitch said sternly. "I saw the dark shadow."

"It's worse than that!" Oki exclaimed.

"What do you mean?" Uncle Griffinskitch asked.

"I can't say for sure," Oki replied. "But the elders have called an emergency meeting, and you're needed right away, Elder Griffinskitch. It's something very serious!"

"I must make greater haste," the old wizard declared. "Kendra, get back home, and mind yourself. I'll be back as soon as I can."

Kendra started to object, but it was clear her uncle wasn't in the mood to argue. Without further fuss, the whiskered Een turned and headed down the path.

"Did you see the shadow, Oki?" Kendra asked as soon as her uncle was out of sight.

"No, but I heard it," Oki told her, seeming to shiver at the very thought of the shadow. "And whatever it was, it made an enormous hole on the lawn in front of the Elder Stone."

"Really?" Kendra said. "This I've got to see."

"I'm not sure that's such a good idea," Oki said.

"Oh, c'mon!" Kendra urged. "It'll be fun. Just follow me. I know a shortcut!"

She turned and disappeared through the blades of grass.

"You know, it's not normal for an Een to seek out adventure," Oki twittered as he reluctantly followed after her.

"Well, you're always telling me that I'm not a normal Een," Kendra called over her shoulder.

"That's true," Oki said. "I'm more Een than you are. I never crave adventure. In my experience, adventure can mean only one thing: danger!"

"Oh, what could happen?" Kendra asked. "It's just a giant hole."

"Exactly," Oki said. "The perfect sort of thing for a tiny mouse like me to fall into."

"Oh, I won't let that happen," Kendra told him, and she quickened her pace across the forest floor. To her, the giant world seemed a peaceful place again. The soft summer light was smiling upon the mushrooms and wildflowers, and she

could almost forget about the dark shadow. But the silence was not to last.

"There's no way I'm going anywhere near that Elder Stone, you slug-brained, foul-winded, barf-infested fur ball!" came a sharp voice.

"Who said that?" Oki squeaked.

"It came from that direction," Kendra said, pointing through the trees.

Just then, they heard a second voice: "I'll have you know you're speaking to Ratchet Ringtail, perhaps the most talented and respected inventor in all the land of Een!"

"More like Ratchet Rattlehead if you ask me!" the first voice retorted.

"Ratchet?" Kendra cried, throwing a startled glance in Oki's direction. "What's he up to now?"

"You can bet it's trouble, whatever it is," Oki said. "You know Ratchet!"

Kendra nodded, for she did indeed know Ratchet—all too well. He was one of her favorite friends, though in truth most Eens looked upon him as a troublemaker. Ratchet the raccoon considered himself an amateur wizard and an inventor with extraordinary talent. No one knew exactly what that meant, though Kendra had long ago come to the belief that Ratchet simply invented with the help of what little magic he thought he knew. His inventions were rarely practical. There were his time boots, for example, with their long toes curling at the ends so that they pointed behind you. The boots were meant to take you back in time and, to Ratchet's credit, they actually worked—sort of. Unfortunately, you kept bumping into yourself coming the other way, so the journey into the past always ended up being a rather short one.

"I just need to work out the kinks," Ratchet had said at the time, though if he ever did, Kendra had never found out. Most of Ratchet's inventions seemed to collect dust on the shelves of his laboratory.

Still, the thing about Ratchet was that he always listened to Kendra. In many ways, he treated her just like an adult. That was worth a lot in Kendra's book, whether he was a wizard, an inventor, or even just a troublesome animal.

"All your friends are animals," Uncle Griffinskitch had told her once.

It was true, of course, but it had never seemed to bother him before Elder Burdock Brown had come by one day and pointed out as much. Burdock had only one eyebrow. It was dark, shaggy, and it stretched across his forehead like an angry caterpillar. Kendra wasn't sure if Burdock was grumpier than her uncle, but he was certainly more expressive. No simple humph would do his opinions justice.

"Simply put, your niece is strange," Kendra had overheard Burdock tell her uncle one day. "It's not normal to be hanging out with animals all the time. They'll turn her into a wild thing."

"Come now, Burdock," Uncle Griffinskitch had said. "You're wilder than most Een animals."

"We're talking about Kendra!" Burdock had snapped. "She's got a mind of her own, that girl."

"Some would say that's a good thing," Uncle Griffinskitch had muttered.

"It's the kind of thing that leads to trouble," Burdock had retorted. "There are strange thoughts floating about that child's mind. I'd be worried if I were you."

Uncle Griffinskitch had only responded with a humph.

"Be that way then," Burdock had grumbled. "But I say she takes after her mother, and that's trouble enough for us all."

"Oh, don't worry about that sour old bore," Ratchet had told her afterwards, when she had come to him in a rage. "I don't care what he says about us animals. As for you, you're all right in my book, Kendra."

And that's why she liked Ratchet. He always made her feel better.

Kendra and Oki scrambled through the tall wildflowers and soon found the raccoon. He was sitting in the middle of a small pumpkin patch, his snout twisted in a fierce scowl. The pumpkins had all been carved with faces, just like jack-o'-lanterns, and were glaring back at Ratchet with scowls even more fierce than his own.

Then, to Kendra's surprise, one of the pumpkins spoke: "What, nothing to say, Rattlehead?"

"I was lost in thought for a moment, if you must know," Ratchet retorted.

"Yes, I'm sure it's unfamiliar territory to you!" the pumpkin hissed.

Just then Ratchet looked up to notice Kendra and Oki.

"Well, hello there, my young friends," the raccoon said with a grin. "I see you have stumbled upon my latest invention."

"Er . . . invention?" Kendra asked. "What exactly are the pumpkins supposed to do?"

"Well, they're my new helpers," Ratchet explained.

"Helpers!" the biggest pumpkin cried. "More like slaves! We didn't sign up for this! Emancipation! We demand emancipation!"

"I don't even know what that means," Ratchet declared.

"It means freedom," Oki piped up. "But what are you going to do with your pumpkin helpers, Ratchet?"

"Well, the first thing I reckon I'll do is use them as boats," Ratchet explained. "You know, I can use them to ferry folks up and down the river."

"How will the boats stay afloat?" Kendra asked. "Won't water pour through their faces?"

"Of course not," Ratchet replied indignantly. "They're magic faces after all."

"Magic! You masked muffin-head!" the nearest pumpkin snickered. "You wouldn't know magic if it nipped you on the tail!"

"What's wrong with your jack-o'-lanterns?" Kendra asked. "They don't seem very . . . er . . . polite."

"Oh, don't worry about them," Ratchet said. "Their bark is worse than their bite."

"And your stench is worse than that," a small yellowish pumpkin told the raccoon. "I've come across Goojuns with sweeter breath than your horrible, fly-maiming, worm-curling odor!"

"I ought to make you all into soup," Ratchet grumbled. "Or maybe a big pie. How about that?"

"Oh yeah?" the biggest of the pumpkins sneered. "How about this?" He puckered his mouth and let the pumpkin seeds fly, spitting them at the raccoon in rapid fire.

"Ouch!" Ratchet cried, as the seeds bounced off his head.

"Maybe you should carve less angry faces in your pumpkins," Oki suggested. "They might not be so rude then."

"Is that so?" Ratchet muttered, gently rubbing his head. "And what do you know about inventing?"

"Never mind that," Kendra interjected. "What about the shadow, Ratchet? Did you see it?"

"Of course," the raccoon replied. "You'd have to be as blind as old Treewort Timm to miss it. Actually, I was just on my way down to the Elder Stone to see what I could find out."

"We had the same idea," Kendra said. "There's a giant hole in the ground that we want to take a look at."

"Well, c'mon on then," Ratchet said. "We'll take one of my boats."

Before Kendra or Oki had time to object, the raccoon turned and began rolling one of the pumpkins down towards the River Wink. The pumpkin, of course, yelled and cursed the whole way, and Ratchet had to keep apologizing over his shoulder to his young friends. Of course, they were more amused than anything else, and it wasn't long before they reached the river's edge.

"Oh, wait a minute," Ratchet said. "I need an oar."

He disappeared into the nearby shrubs and soon reappeared with a long pole. "This will do," he said.

"How do we get in?" Oki asked Ratchet.

"We just have to remove the lid," the raccoon replied. Grabbing hold of the pumpkin's twisted stem, he removed the roof of the large boat, and the three friends clambered inside.

"You're all too fat," the pumpkin complained. "We're sure to sink, you bloated blobs of blubber. Emancipation! I demand emancipation."

"Oh, just behave yourself," Ratchet warned. He used the pole to push off from the shore, and they were soon on their way down the River Wink.

CHAPTER 3

S A ecret Door

For those of you who don't know, the River Wink leads straight past the largest town in the land of Een, and that's the town of Faun's End. It's here where you will find the Elder Stone, though I regret to say that, being from the outside world, you'll probably have a hard time finding the land of Een at all, let alone the town of Faun's End. Nonetheless, if you ever do find your way to this enchanted country, then you should certainly visit the Elder Stone, for it is a magnificent place indeed.

Kendra and her friends in the jack-o'-lantern boat could see the stone long before they

19

actually reached it, for it towered above the Een shops and homes like a castle. And yet it was unlike any castle that Kendra had ever read about, for it had not been built with several bricks or stones but with only one: a single gray rock that thrust towards the sky as if it were trying to touch the distant clouds.

Legend held that the Elder Stone had taken hundreds of years to complete. This was no surprise, for the inside had been hollowed out and tunneled with countless rooms and passageways, while much of the outside was carved with tiny stone pictures of stars, animals, and strange Een faces with all manners of expression. Some of the faces framed tiny windows and doorways while others gazed upon the distant ground with long open mouths that gushed sparkling waterfalls. These falls glistened in the sunlight, changing color as they tumbled down the Elder Stone from ledge to ledge, spilling at last into a narrow moat that surrounded the rock's base. From here, a series of pumps and pipes returned the water to the top of the stone, so that the frolicking water might repeat its journey.

Kendra loved the waterfalls of the Elder Stone. She could stare at them for hours, watching them change from blue to green, then indigo, red, orange, and yellow in turn. Indeed, she was watching them now and was almost in a trance when Ratchet's pumpkin boat clunked against the shore of the River Wink.

"We're here," Ratchet announced.

"I thought there'd be a whole crowd here," Kendra said. "But we're the only ones."

"You know Een folk," Ratchet said, helping Kendra and Oki out of the pumpkin. "They're scared of their own shadows. I imagine that big, dark shape was enough to send most Eens hiding under their beds."

"I'm an Een, and I'm not hiding under my bed," Kendra pointed out.

"Well, you're no normal Een," Ratchet said. "I suspect we'll find your whiskers yet, and then we'll know for sure you're a critter, just like one of us."

"Oh, Ratchet," Kendra giggled.

"Well, let's go check this hole out," the raccoon said, as he tied the boat to a nearby tree root.

"I would love to knot you to a tree," the jack-o'-lantern boat told Ratchet.

"If you weren't so grumpy, I might let you come with us," Ratchet retorted.

"No thanks," the pumpkin growled. "Spending more than five seconds around you fills me with a burning desire to be alone."

"Come on," Ratchet said to Kendra and Oki. "Let's get out of here before this exchange gets any uglier."

"It couldn't possibly get uglier than you, you wandering waste of fur," the pumpkin hollered after them.

"I really don't know what I did wrong," Ratchet confessed to his friends as they approached the stone. "Jack-o'-lantern boats seemed like such a good idea yesterday. Of course, that was before I knew pumpkins were obsessed with constipation."

"No, not constipation!" Oki squeaked. "*Emancipation.*"

"No one wants constipation," Kendra told Ratchet with a giggle.

"Well, how do you know?" Ratchet asked crossly. He didn't like to be shown a fool, but Kendra patted him on his back, and he quickly forgot his embarrassment.

They soon came to the giant hole that Oki had told them about. The pit was deep and dark, with ragged edges and large chunks of dirt and grass scattered about its gaping mouth. It was as if someone—or something—had violently plunged right through the earth.

"I'd sure like to know what made this mess," Ratchet said with a low whistle.

Kendra peered over the edge of the hole, her braids hanging into the blackness. "I wonder where it goes," she mused.

"I know a way to find out," Ratchet said. "We have to get into that council meeting."

"Oh, we can't do that," Oki said quickly. "It's a private meeting."

"Well, you work for the elders," Ratchet said. "They have to let you in."

"I'm just a lowly messenger mouse," Oki protested.

"C'mon," Ratchet persisted. "We'll sneak in then."

"That would be spying," Oki pointed out.

"Good," Ratchet said. "It's been a long time since I've stirred up that sort of trouble."

"Oh, dear," Oki murmured, and Kendra knew there would no use arguing with Ratchet. The raccoon would just pester Oki until he got his way.

With a sigh, the tiny mouse turned and led his two friends across one of the bridges that spanned the moat to the Elder Stone. Oki was just about to knock on the front door when it suddenly flew open, and they found themselves face-to-face with Juniper Jinx, captain of the Een guard and protector of the elders. Even though Jinx was a grasshopper (and thus smaller than both Kendra and Oki), her reputation made her seem larger than a giant. With her long hind legs and ever-ready sword, she was known as a fierce fighter, and few dared to challenge her.

"What do you want?" Jinx demanded.

"We . . . er, Oki forgot something inside the hall," Kendra stammered.

"Too bad for you, Oki!" Jinx said. "You'll have to get your 'something' later. There's a very important meeting about to take place."

"But Oki works for the elders," Ratchet said. "You can let him in."

"Nice try," Jinx snorted. "But working part-time after school delivering messages for the elders doesn't give Oki the right to attend this meeting. Or you, for that matter, Ringtail."

Kendra could see Ratchet's face twist with anger. She knew what the raccoon was thinking—and so did Jinx.

"Go ahead and try it, Ringtail," Jinx said. "You think you can wrestle your way past me? Ha! You'll be lying on the ground with the point of my sword pinned through your tail faster than you can blink an eye!"

Ratchet grunted, but Kendra knew he wouldn't push the matter. Despite her smallness, no one in the land of Een was stronger than Jinx. Oki had once told Kendra that the reason Jinx was so strong was that she had accidentally swallowed a magic healing potion. Kendra wondered how a healing potion could give you super strength. But there was no denying that

Jinx was the toughest critter this side of the curtain.

"Now scram!" Jinx ordered, turning smartly on her heel and slamming the door in Ratchet's face. They heard it lock with a loud click.

"How do you like that?" Ratchet grumbled.

"C'mon," Kendra said. "There has to be another way into the tower, right Oki?"

"Why are you asking me?" the timid mouse asked.

"Because you work here," Ratchet said, jabbing his paw at the mouse. "And you're too honest to lie. Isn't that why your nickname is 'Honest Oki'? So tell us a way in."

Oki gave his whiskery chin a nervous scratch.

"Don't you want to know what's going on?" Kendra asked.

"Okay, okay," the mouse said finally. "Follow me."

He looked quickly about to make sure no one was watching them, then climbed up to a narrow ledge a few feet from the ground. Kendra and Ratchet looked at each other in puzzlement.

"He's *your* friend," Ratchet told Kendra.

"He knows what he's doing," Kendra said loyally. "C'mon!"

They hurried after the tiny mouse and soon found themselves beside one of the stone's many waterfalls. It sparkled before them, changing colors as it spilled over the mysterious carvings in the wall.

"Now what?" Ratchet asked.

"Just keep your voice down," Oki warned. "The waterfall is a secret door into the Elder Stone."

"Oh, that's easy enough," Ratchet said.

He turned and marched blindly into the tumbling water. He had only taken two short steps, however, when Kendra and Oki suddenly heard a loud "Ouch!" and the raccoon fell straight back on his tail. He was drenched from head to foot but had nothing to show for the shower except a bruised nose.

"What happened?" Kendra asked.

"I hit a brick wall, that's what," Ratchet scowled. "What kind of trick are you trying to pull, Oki?"

"You didn't let me finish," the mouse squeaked. "It's a secret entrance, you know. You have to wait until the waterfall turns blue of course!"

With that, Oki turned and stepped straight through the waterfall, just as it changed from green to blue.

"There's a trick!" Kendra said excitedly.

"Well, here goes nothing," Ratchet muttered, this time stepping into the waterfall more cautiously.

Kendra waited until the tip of the raccoon's tail disappeared through the water. Then she quickly skipped after him, her mind racing with thoughts of adventure.

CHAPTER 4
Into the Elder Stone

If you have any experience with castles or dungeons, you will know that they are dark places, often a maze of twisted passageways and winding staircases, where it is all too easy to get lost. The Elder Stone was no different, and it was only Oki's knowledge of the mighty rock that allowed our friends to find their way. The tiny mouse lifted a torch from the wall and led Kendra and Ratchet quietly but surely through the crooked corridors and shadowy rooms of the rock.

At last, he came to a stop before a plain wooden door. He opened it with a gentle nudge of his paw, and the band of would-be spies found themselves in a small room with a swatch of red curtain drawn across the far wall.

"On the other side of that curtain is the council chamber where the elders meet," Oki whispered. "All we have to do is hide here, and we'll be able to hear their every word."

Kendra and her friends poked their noses through the curtain and gazed upon the chamber. It was small and circular, and it was dimly lit by a few flickering torches set in the wall. In the very center of the room there was a small glistening pool, and around one side of the pool were seven seats, placed there for the elders. Most of them had already taken their places, including Uncle Griffinskitch and the ornery Burdock Brown. Kendra recognized the other elders as well: Becka Bluebell, Enid Evermoon, Skarab Strom, and Nora Neverfar.

"They're just awaiting Winter Woodsong, leader of the council," Oki whispered. "As soon as she arrives, the meeting will begin."

These words had no sooner left Oki's lips when Captain Jinx marched into the room and in a highly official voice, announced: "Make way for the eldest of the elders, Winter Woodsong, leader of the council!"

The elders had been engaged in hushed whispers, but they immediately fell silent and turned their heads towards a small door in the far corner of the room. After a moment the door slowly creaked open and there appeared a tiny Een, so white and frail that she made Uncle Griffinskitch seem as spry and able as a spring chicken. Kendra had never seen Winter Woodsong before, but there was no mistaking Winter's nobility and grace. She leaned heavily on a twisted wooden staff and drew labored breaths as she walked. Deep wrinkles lined her round face, and her clear blue eyes glim-

mered with friendly wisdom, the kind that Kendra imagined a grandmother or favorite aunt would have. (Kendra herself, however, had never known any relative other than Uncle Griffinskitch.)

"Welcome all," Winter greeted as she took her seat among the elders. "I apologize for calling this urgent meeting. But the unthinkable has happened. A monster from the outside world has breached the magic curtain of Een."

A gasp went across the room. The elders looked at each other, bewildered and speechless.

"That's impossible!" Burdock Brown exclaimed, his one dark eyebrow twisting and arching on his furrowed brow. "Only Eens and Een animals can go through the curtain!"

"You have all seen the terrible hole," Winter said. "No inhabitant of Een could have ripped such a black pit through the earth."

"I saw the shadow of this wretched creature," Uncle Griffinskitch remarked in his deep, gravelly voice. "But I know not what it was."

"Nor I," Winter said. "That is why I have asked Professor Bumblebean to join our meeting. Hopefully, he will be able to shed some light on this mystery."

With this announcement, a tall, thin Een stepped forward into the circle of elders.

"I've never seen that funny-looking fellow before," Ratchet whispered from behind the curtain.

"That's because you never go to the library," Oki said. "Bumblebean is probably one of the smartest Eens around. Winter has a great deal of respect for him. She's always calling him to speak to the elders. But other than that, I don't think he leaves the Een library very much."

Kendra didn't have any trouble believing Oki, for Professor Bumblebean certainly had the look of someone who didn't like to spend much time outdoors. His skin was pale and his clothes, though rumpled, showed little wear and tear. A pair of half-moon glasses dangled precariously on the end of his large nose. But despite this, the professor squinted continually, suggesting long hours spent at study. His smile was friendly enough, however, and Kendra couldn't help but take a liking to the strange Een.

"Unfortunately, I have little to report," Professor Bumblebean announced to the elders. "I have conducted a thorough investigation of the chasm, but I'm afraid I have yet to determine the nature of our intruder."

"What did he say?" Kendra asked Oki from their hiding place.

"Oh, don't mind him," Oki whispered back. "He always talks like that. Bumblebean's rather fond of big words. All he said was that he doesn't know anything."

"Some report you have for us," Burdock grumbled to his fellow elders.

"Well, I do say," Professor Bumblebean stammered. "I have had little time to examine the scene of this incident. But I can assure you, this was an immense beast. It certainly was not your average monster."

"No kidding," Burdock snapped. "You don't have to be a bookworm to know that. All you had to do was hear its scream."

"We must mind our tempers," Winter declared. "This mystery has us all on edge. And I'm afraid there is more bad news yet."

"What could be worse than an intruder?" Becka Bluebell asked anxiously.

"It's what the intruder came for," Winter replied. "The Box of Whispers."

Again, a gasp went through the council.

"What the heck is the Box of Whispers?" Ratchet whispered to Kendra and Oki from their hiding place.

"I don't know," Oki admitted. "I've never heard of it."

Kendra frowned. Maybe Oki had never heard of the box, but it was obviously important. Staring out the curtain, Kendra could see that every last one of the elders looked shaken and pale, including her uncle.

"We . . . we should not mention the box in the presence of Captain Jinx and Professor Bumblebean," Enid Evermoon murmured. "They are not elders."

"We shall keep the contents of the box a secret," Winter assured the council. "But I'm afraid we must speak of the box itself."

"Why?" Nora Neverfar asked nervously. "What has become of it?"

Winter looked gravely around the circle. "I'm afraid the box, and the magic key that opens it, has been stolen," she said finally. At once the chamber erupted in an explosion of frenzied voices.

"That's impossible!"

"How could this happen?"

"Days of Een!"

"The oldest and most important Een treasure—gone!"

"Yes," Winter murmured, once the room had quieted down. "The box is gone, stolen right from the vault that lies beneath the Elder Stone. Nothing else did the beast take. Only the box and the key."

"Een is in terrible danger!" Nora Neverfar cried. "If the box is opened—"

"The Box of Whispers hasn't been opened in over a thousand years!" Uncle Griffinskitch boomed.

"But if it *is* opened," Nora said, "well . . . the results could be disastrous."

"Why?" Ratchet whispered to Kendra behind the curtain. "What will happen?"

Kendra had no idea, but before she could tell Ratchet as much, their attention was turned back to the elders.

"And will this thief be able to open the box, even with the

key?" Burdock demanded. "The box contains magic of the oldest kind. The ancients enchanted it with spells that not even I understand."

"That's a chance we can't take," Uncle Griffinskitch said, stroking his whiskers.

"I cannot speak of the box itself, for its existence has been unknown to me until this very moment," Professor Bumblebean piped up. "As to our thief, it may have been aided by an Een; that might be one way it could have slipped past the magic curtain."

"No Een can help a monster from the outside world," Burdock said crossly. "Our code forbids it. To help a monster means to be expelled from the land of Een forever!"

"Still, the box has been stolen," Winter said. "We don't know how, and we don't know why. But one thing is clear: we *must* recover it."

"How?" Burdock asked sourly. "Where do we even begin to look?"

"The situation is grave," Winter said. "We need help. We must consult the magic orb."

"Days of Een!" Uncle Griffinskitch cried. "The council has never called forth the orb during my watch."

"But we shall call it now," Winter said. "For we have need of its wisdom. Does anyone disagree?"

A chorus of "no's" echoed through the chamber.

"Humph," Uncle Griffinskitch added. It was a quiet type of humph, one filled with anxiety and discomfort.

CHAPTER 5

Winter Woodsong Calls the Orb

You have probably never seen a Faerie, Elf, or some similar creature call upon a magic spell. It is quite a wonderful sight to behold—let me assure you. For one thing, it is quite surprising to think that something so small can be so powerful. But such is the nature of Faeries, Elves, and even Eens. As for Winter Woodsong, she was one of the most powerful Eens in all the land, so you can imagine that Kendra and her friends watched with eager anticipation when the eldest of the elders closed her eyes and began to hum.

The hum was a magical sound, unlike anything Kendra had ever heard. It came deep from within Winter's throat, loud and with a tremor, like a thousand hummingbirds beating their tiny wings all at once. As the sound in Winter's throat grew louder, the pool in the middle of the room began to bubble and sparkle. Then, with a soft "whoosh" sound, a stream of water shot into the air, and out of its midst appeared a glowing crystal orb. It floated magically in the air, whirling with a quiet buzz as stars and bolts of electricity crackled about its surface. The room filled with a deep purple light. Then, softly, the orb spoke.

"Why have I been disturbed from my slumber?" it asked. "I have slept now for years longer than any could number."

"I, leader of the Council of Elders, have called forth your wisdom, O Gracious One," Winter said. "We need your guidance, for the Box of Whispers has been stolen."

The orb did not reply immediately. It spun swiftly in the air, buzzing more loudly now, as if it were in deep thought. At last it said: "The Box of Whispers is the oldest treasure of Een, created in ancient times, long since seen. Safely, it has rested for decades untold. If not returned, our safety may unfold."

"And where is the box now?" Uncle Griffinskitch asked.

The orb spun again for another moment, then said, "Deep in the castle of Krodos the box now resides. There, the Red Thief lives. In vengeful ecstasy, he writhes."

Kendra saw Winter and her uncle exchange a nervous glance. Then Winter asked the orb, "And who is this 'Red Thief'?"

"Many creatures live beyond the curtain," the orb said. "The thief is one of these—this is certain."

Winter frowned at the orb's mysterious answer. "What will we do in this matter?" she asked next.

"Set forth on a quest, some brave Eens must," the glowing crystal replied. "With but a select few this task we trust. First, to Gregor Griffinskitch I cast my light, to lead the way with his magical might!"

At that moment, a light beamed forth from the orb and shone upon the old and whiskered Een. If Uncle Griffinskitch was surprised by the orb's announcement, he didn't show it. Without hesitation, he stepped forward into the middle of the chamber.

"Next, I call forth Broon Bumblebean, most learned of any scholar," the orb continued. "Then, Juniper Jinx, take your place to protect the Eens with sword and steely pace!"

Jinx and Professor Bumblebean both stepped forward to join Uncle Griffinskitch. The orb paused, and a whisper went through the rest of the council. Who else would join the company?

Then, without warning, the orb suddenly turned towards the red curtain where Kendra and her friends were hiding.

The orb shot out another ray of light. The curtain fluttered, then flew wide open, revealing the spies for all to see.

"What is the meaning of this?" Burdock demanded. "Intruders! We have intruders!"

"Silence!" Winter insisted. "The orb speaks yet."

"Come forth, little Oki, both honest and true," the orb declared. "With your purest mind this quest pursue!"

Kendra noticed sweat pouring down Oki's face. She knew the last thing he wanted to do was step into the middle of the room, but it seemed as if the orb was controlling his very legs. Trembling head to foot, he joined the others who had been named.

"Last, I call Kendra Kandlestar to the floor," the orb said. "With spark of courage, your choices will roar. Now, I have said all I have to say. Go forth, friends, and save the day."

With these final words, the orb retreated into the pool, leaving the five chosen heroes to stand uncomfortably in the chamber.

"I go where Kendra goes," Ratchet declared, marching into the middle of the elders. "I don't care what that orb says."

"Humph," Uncle Griffinskitch mumbled angrily. "What right do you have to demand anything?"

"Indeed!" Burdock added, pounding his staff. "Ratchet Ringtail, you are nothing more than a spy, a scoundrel, and—above all else—a troublemaker!"

"You forgot inventor," Ratchet added boldly. "A world-class one."

"Only an animal would think to spy on the Council of Elders," Burdock hissed.

"Now, now, Burdock," Elder Nora Neverfar said. "There is an Eenling in their group, too, you know."

"She might as well be an animal," Burdock snorted. "She's acting like one."

"At ease, elders," Winter said, kindly raising her gentle hand. The orb had taxed her powers, but still, she spoke with firmness. "Indeed, they should not have been listening to our private words. But perhaps they were called here by some magic power, for the orb has named them for this quest. Two of them at least."

"Well, like I said, I go where my pals go," Ratchet repeated.

"The company of heroes has been chosen," Winter decreed. "And so it must be, five in all. No more, no less shall go. That includes you, I'm afraid, Mr. Ringtail."

"I don't like this one bit," Ratchet said. "I think that orb just forgot to name me. Call it back, why don't you?"

"The whole idea of this quest is ridiculous," Burdock Brown interjected. "No one has been beyond the magic curtain since . . . since . . ." He paused uncomfortably and Kendra couldn't help but notice the rest of the elders staring at her.

"Ahem," Uncle Griffinskitch grunted, breaking the silence.

"Well, it has been ten years," Burdock muttered. "Do you really think it's wise to go into the outside world?"

"Do we dare go against the orb's word?" Enid Evermoon asked.

"No, of course not," Winter repeated. "The orb has spoken. That will be all."

"But I can't go!" Oki squeaked. Kendra knew Oki well enough to know that he had been trying to contain his fear, but now everything gushed out at once. "I don't know anything about magic quests! And my parents will never let me go! Eek!"

Winter smiled kindly upon the tiny mouse. "Little one," she said, "you *will* go on the quest. This is not a matter for discussion. As for your parents, I will speak to them myself and do my best to ease their fears."

Oki gave Kendra a helpless look, but all she could do was shrug. She felt just as powerless. Why had the orb cho-

sen her? She had no special talent or skill. She wasn't a wizard, a professor, or a captain. The choice of Oki made sense. He had worked after school for the elders for over a year and seemed to know all sorts of things. But what help could she, Kendra, be on such a long and dangerous journey? And why had everyone stared at her when the magic curtain had been mentioned? What did the curtain have to do with her?

Then Winter spoke, breaking Kendra's dizzying train of thought.

"Gregor, come forth, old friend," the eldest of the elders called to Uncle Griffinskitch.

The old wizard shuffled forth and bowed his head before Winter.

"A heavy task has been laid upon you," Winter stated sternly, but not unkindly.

"I am ready for it, Elder Woodsong," Uncle Griffinskitch told her.

"Then I trust you are clear about this mission," Winter said. "The Box of Whispers is what you seek, Gregor. All other interests must be cast aside."

"I understand all too well," the old Een said, and Kendra caught a hint of sadness in his voice. She wondered what Winter had meant by her comment. What else did Winter think Uncle Griffinskitch would want to do out in the wilds beyond the magic curtain?

"Old friend," Winter said, leaning forward to rest her hand on Uncle Griffinskitch's shoulder, "come to my study before the moon rises tonight. I will consult with you further, in private, before you set forth on this quest."

"I will come," Uncle Griffinskitch said.

"Very well," Winter said, turning her attention back to the room. "Then the council is dismissed. Our meeting is ended."

"But—," Burdock began.

"There will be no more discussion on the matter," Winter said firmly. "Council shall take leave immediately. We must let the company prepare for its quest to recover the Box of Whispers!"

CHAPTER 6

The Garden of Books

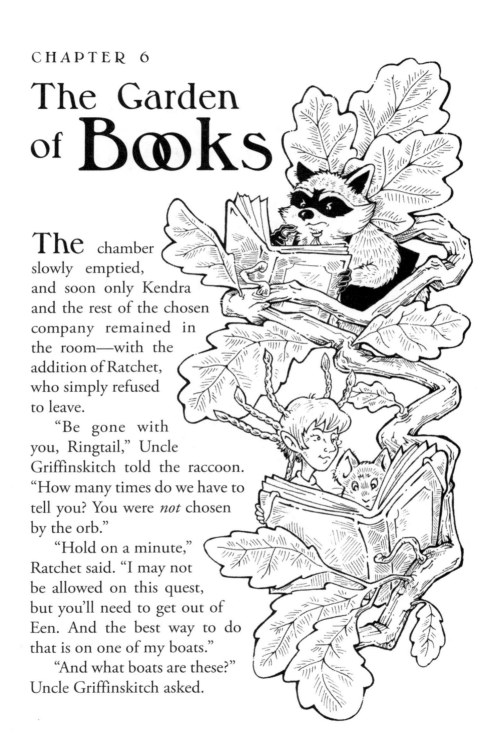

The chamber slowly emptied, and soon only Kendra and the rest of the chosen company remained in the room—with the addition of Ratchet, who simply refused to leave.

"Be gone with you, Ringtail," Uncle Griffinskitch told the raccoon. "How many times do we have to tell you? You were *not* chosen by the orb."

"Hold on a minute," Ratchet said. "I may not be allowed on this quest, but you'll need to get out of Een. And the best way to do that is on one of my boats."

"And what boats are these?" Uncle Griffinskitch asked.

"Oh, they're his new invention," Kendra said. As far as she was concerned, the longer that Ratchet was with them on the journey, the better. "They're great," she added timidly, noting her uncle's annoyed glance.

"Humph," Uncle Griffinskitch muttered. It was the type of humph that meant he was deep in thought. "Your boats may be of some service," he said after a moment. "But you will go no further than the curtain. Is that clear?"

"Of course," Ratchet replied.

"Then be ready to leave at dawn," the old wizard instructed. "The sooner we leave, the sooner we'll rescue the box."

"And the sooner we can come back home," Oki whispered to Kendra.

"I do say, Elder Griffinskitch," Professor Bumblebean said, pushing his half-moon glasses up the slope of his nose, "no Een I know has been beyond the magic curtain for ten years. As such, we should visit the Een library."

"What for?" Jinx asked.

"Why, we have maps and books and journals of the ancient explorers housed there," Professor Bumblebean replied. "We can't possibly commence this journey without them."

Jinx rolled her eyes. "Well, I have my sword. That'll do for me."

"Humph," Uncle Griffinskitch muttered. "Books and swords may serve us well on our journey, but we'll need other things as well."

"Like what?" Kendra asked. She had never been on any journey, long or otherwise, and she had no idea how to pre-pare herself.

"We'll need sleeping gear, warm clothing, and some dried foodstuff," Uncle Griffinskitch replied. "Remember, we've got a long way to go, and everything we bring will have to be carried on our own backs."

It all felt a little overwhelming to Kendra. Once again, she found herself questioning the orb's decision to include her on the quest. But her uncle must have noticed a look of exasperation on her face for he tapped her on the shoulder.

"Don't fret," he told her. "I must go meet with Elder Woodsong, but tonight, I will help you pack. And Oki, I will pass by your house on my way home and leave instructions with your parents. In the meantime, I suggest that you all go with the professor and help him in the library."

"I'll stay out of this book business," Jinx declared. "My weapons need sharpening before we set off."

"Very well," Uncle Griffinskitch said. "Attend to your affairs, Captain Jinx. We'll meet you back here at dawn."

Jinx nodded and took her leave. Uncle Griffinskitch grunted his own farewell and hobbled away to meet with Winter Woodsong.

"Well, we're off to the library," Professor Bumblebean said cheerfully, leading Kendra, Oki, and Ratchet out of the Elder Stone and into the streets of Faun's End.

In Kendra's opinion, there was no other building in all of Een like the library. For starters, it was made from a giant barrel. To human eyes, the barrel would have seemed gigantic, but to Kendra, it was simply enormous—an alien, oversized object from a world she found difficult to imagine. Even so, the barrel was not the only reason the library seemed so spectacular. At the top of the great casket, the ancient Eens had raised an enormous crystal dome, built of sparkling glass and arched branches that twisted and snaked to meet at a sharp point high above the ground.

"It's marvelous, is it not?" Professor Bumblebean beamed as he brought the group to a stop on the wide steps that led into the library. "This structure represents one of the most fascinating feats of architecture in all of Een."

"Is it very old?" Kendra asked.

"Oh, indeed," the professor replied, seeming all too pleased that she had asked. "Do you not know the story of the library? You see, it was my ancestor, the legendary Byron Bumblebean, who was responsible for the beginnings of the library. Byron once traveled to a distance land of giants, where he engaged in a crooked game of cards with a gargantuan scoundrel. Despite the cheating nature of giants, Byron won the match. When his colossal opponent could not pay his bet, he gave Byron a barrel of pickles. Well, as the story goes, when he finished eating all the pickles, he donated the empty barrel to Faun's End, and the town used it to build the library."

"Sounds like the ancient Eens really got themselves out of a pickle," Ratchet said, and Kendra and Oki started to giggle.

"I'm not sure I understand your meaning," Professor Bumblebean said, puffing out his chest with pride.

"It was just a joke," Ratchet said.

"A joke?" Professor Bumblebean asked. "I don't see the fun in it. Myself, I descend from a long line of scholars, and I believe I would know if something were funny."

"Okay, okay," Ratchet muttered. "There's no need to get your knickers in a twist. Let's just get on with our business."

"My word," the professor said, rolling his eyes and turning towards the tall arched door of the library. "No wonder Elder Burdock is always referring to you as a scalawag."

"What's a scalawag?" Kendra whispered to Oki as they followed Professor Bumblebean.

"I think it's the same as a rascal," Oki replied.

The professor opened the mighty wooden door of the library. The door swung inward with a creak, revealing a vast and magical interior. Kendra gasped. No matter how many times she visited the library, she never failed to be awed. Eens, you see, aren't the type to clutter their libraries with racks and shelves and such. And why would they? Book trees do just as well, if not better, as long as you can find the seeds. Of course, there's no shortage of such seeds in Een, and the library seemed more a garden than a place of study. And what a garden! It bore no fruit or flowers, but books—more than you can imagine—with each tree sprouting forth with wonderful volumes of text.

The trees stretched up to the domed roof of the library. (Thankfully, book trees are small—Een-sized, if you will—

and fit snugly.) Staircases spiraled up many of the trees so that the taller branches could be reached, and there were many balconies and galleries suspended high above the main floor. The space was warm and inviting, for sunshine filtered through the dome and the fragrance from the trees was delightful.

"Ah," Professor Bumblebean said, taking a deep breath, "the glorious aroma of knowledge. Well, come now, we'll ascend to the section on creatures from beyond the magic curtain."

As they crossed the floor, they could see a great many Eens bustling about the book trees.

Ratchet expressed amazement that the Eens were still at work after seeing the dark shadow, but Kendra wasn't so surprised. Eens may be easily startled, she knew, but they were also just as happy to forget any danger as soon as possible. "Out of sight, out of mind," she had heard many of her Een teachers say, and now she watched as the library workers happily went about their tasks. One Een was darting among the orchard groves with a large watering can, though it contained not water, as you may suppose, but rather, all the letters of the alphabet. The cheerful fellow whistled as he sprinkled the letters on the roots of the trees. Another Een was ripping pages out of a small book and tossing them into a hole, which was being dug by two of his co-workers.

"What are they doing, Professor?" Kendra asked.

"I do say!" Professor Bumblebean remarked. "Everyone knows that's how you plant a new book tree."

They passed another row of trees, and here they saw still more Eens at work. These were each sitting beneath a different tree, with their eyes closed and their hands stretched out to touch the trunks. They seemed in some sort of trance.

Before Kendra could ask the question on the tip of her tongue, Professor Bumblebean had an answer for her. "They're fertilizing the trees with knowledge," he announced.

At last the professor brought them to a tree in the very center of the room. A staircase snaked around its trunk, winding ever upwards.

"The section we are about to visit is normally restricted to the elders and other important Eens," the professor declared. "I hope you respect the privilege you are about to enjoy."

He turned and led them up the staircase. It was a long way up. Kendra wanted to pause and peer down upon the library, but Professor Bumblebean kept such a steady pace that she had no time to linger.

At last, the stairway came to an end at a small wooden door, framed with the lush leaves of the very tree they had just climbed. Professor Bumblebean whispered a password, and the door opened inward, revealing a quiet balcony that stretched across the uppermost heights of the dome. The tops of the book trees arched over the long gallery, creating a pleasant green canopy.

"Here we are," the professor said. "Some of the oldest and tallest trees, containing our most ancient knowledge, reach here. Now, I will attend to some maps. The rest of you search for books about monsters."

"What type of monsters?" Oki asked.

"All of them, of course," the professor announced. "We may encounter all sorts of creatures on this journey."

"I was afraid he'd say that," Oki told his friends.

Together, Kendra, Oki, and Ratchet set about to explore the gallery. They could see that many of the books were not yet ripe; these were green and closed, their knowledge not yet ready to be read. Other books had blossomed and were eagerly displaying their crisp white pages, inviting the young friends to delight in their words.

"Oh, here's a good one!" Ratchet declared, calling Kendra and Oki over to a small yellowish book. The raccoon flipped through the pages, only to have a jet of fire shoot out at his face. "Yeesh!" Ratchet cried. "How do you like that business?"

"Careful," Professor Bumblebean said, rushing over and wrenching the book out of Ratchet's paws. He closed the book and saw the word "dragons" printed in large capital letters across the cover. "I do say, of all the books to try to open!" the professor scolded. "This volume hasn't matured yet. It's very dangerous to go opening books that are still trying to grow their text. The books themselves often possess the characteristics of their subjects, you know. If you had paid more attention in school, you'd know this, Ratchet Ringtail."

"It's a good thing you didn't find a book about tornadoes," Kendra said, laughing. "You'd be blown to the end of the earth, and we'd have to go rescue you on top of everything else!"

"Yeesh," Ratchet muttered again, caressing his singed whiskers. "I think I'll let you look for the books from now on, Kendra."

CHAPTER 7

Dinner with Uncle Griffinskitch

In the end, Professor Bumblebean selected more than a dozen books to take with him on the quest. These covered a wide variety of topics and had titles such as *The Illustrated History of Krodos* and *The Comparative Book of Creatures from Beyond the Magic Curtain.* By the time the professor had picked the last book, it was getting quite late, and Kendra had to scamper to make it home before dark.

Despite her haste, the moon was just beginning to cast its crescent smile upon the sky when Kendra turned the last corner in the path and came upon the cottage where she lived with Uncle Griffinskitch. The house was round and squat, encircling the trunk of an ancient yew tree. To Kendra, it seemed as if the tree grew right out of the roof. It was the very core of the cottage, and she could even see its trunk from the inside, for no interior wall had been built to separate the dwelling from the tree. When she was walking through the cottage, Kendra often ran her hand over the bark. It seemed magical to her.

As for the house itself, well, if you have ever been to a wizard's home, you know that they are normally cluttered and somewhat untidy. Uncle Griffinskitch's house was no exception. It was cozy and old, decorated with furniture that had carvings of strange wooden faces, and dusty paintings that told the stories of Een in days long forgotten. The house had many floors and rooms, though several of these could be reached only by enchanted doors and secret passwords. It was in these rooms where Uncle Griffinskitch kept his telescopes, books, cauldrons, and other enchanted items.

When Kendra stepped into the house, Uncle Griffinskitch had already returned from his private meeting with Winter Woodsong. He was sitting at the kitchen table, his nose buried deep in a large book. Without bothering to lift his eyes from his manuscript, the old wizard spoke to her. "How many times have I told you to come home before dark?" he grumbled.

"Well, I was with Bumblebean, after all," Kendra said.

"Professor Bumblebean," Uncle Griffinskitch corrected gruffly.

Kendra noticed a heap of carrot peelings on the table, next to her uncle's elbow. On the hearth, a pot simmered softly, bubbling orange.

"Oh! The giant carrots," Kendra said.

"Hmmm?" Uncle Griffinskitch muttered, finally raising his eyes from his book. "Oh, yes. I was able to reverse your badly placed spell and thought we would have carrot soup for dinner. Though I was beginning to wonder if you were ever going to arrive."

Uncle Griffinskitch rose slowly and dished out the soup. Kendra quickly washed up and joined him for dinner.

The old wizard was quiet, even by his standards, and Kendra began to feel uncomfortable.

"Uncle Griffinskitch?" she asked, finally breaking the awkward silence.

"Hmm," her uncle grunted, slurping his soup.

"What exactly is the Box of Whispers?" she asked. "How come I've never heard of it?"

"It is a matter for elders only," the old Een replied simply.

"But what's in it?" Kendra persisted.

"Once again," Uncle Griffinskitch said, "a matter for elders only."

"Oh," Kendra murmured, staring down at her soup. "But why did everyone look at me when Elder Brown mentioned the magic curtain?"

Uncle Griffinskitch paused, his spoon lifted halfway to his mouth. For a long time he said nothing, and Kendra could see him shift uncomfortably. "You are full of questions tonight," he grumbled. "More so than usual."

"Please," Kendra implored. "Why doesn't Elder Brown like me?"

"Humph," Uncle Griffinskitch grunted. "It's not that. He was referring to your . . . to your family. Your brother and your parents."

"But they died," Kendra said. "A long time ago. When I was just a baby."

Uncle Griffinskitch stroked his whiskers, as if he were in deep thought. "Yes, Kendra," he said finally. "Most likely."

"What do you mean 'most likely'?" Kendra asked, leaning forward across the table. "They might still be alive?"

"I doubt it," Uncle Griffinskitch murmured. "They disappeared beyond the magic curtain. No one knows for sure what happened."

"Disappeared!" Kendra cried. "So they could be alive."

"Humph," Uncle Griffinskitch muttered. "It's doubtful." He lifted his spoon to continue with his supper. But Kendra noticed that he wasn't really eating, just sort of holding the spoon in his hand and staring into his bowl.

Kendra didn't feel so hungry anymore. After a moment she said, "Do you think we will find them? Outside the curtain?"

Uncle Griffinskitch suddenly looked very tired. "If they were alive, I'm sure they would have come back a long time ago. Listen, Kendra. Even though your mother was so much younger than I, we were still very close. You don't know how hard I searched for her and the rest of your family. But you were just a baby then, and ultimately, I had to look after you. I wish we could continue looking, but . . ."

"But what?" Kendra prompted.

"It's the Box of Whispers we need to find," the old wizard said, a tone of reluctance in his voice. "That and that alone."

Kendra stared at her uncle, questions still burning in her mind.

"Maybe you should go start packing your things," Uncle Griffinskitch said. "I'll be up shortly."

Kendra slid off her chair and climbed the stairs to her room. Halfway up, she paused and stared at the painting that hung there of her family. They were all in it—her mother, her father, her brother Kiro, and even Kendra herself, a tiny baby, wrapped in a green blanket, with tiny braids poking out of her head. She sighed. She could never seem to get her uncle to talk about her family. But why?

She stared at the painting for a moment more, then went on to her room. Sometimes she felt guilty for not missing her family more. But how could she miss them? She couldn't even remember them. In many ways, they weren't even real to her. Oh sure, she sometimes dreamed about them, wondered what it would be like to live with them instead of old Uncle Griffinskitch. Would her mom be grouchy like him? Kendra didn't think so. She imagined her as a cheerful and kind mother. And what about the rest of her family? Would she like her brother? Or would she fight with him like Oki always fought with his little sisters?

Once in her room, Kendra began pulling out belongings and stacking them on her small bed. Where to begin? The most important thing, she decided, was to be warm, so she started with her long green cloak, throwing it around her shoulders and taking a look at herself in the mirror.

"Do I look like an adventurer?" she asked her reflection and then shrugged. She didn't even know what an adventurer should look like.

She began collecting other articles of clothing that she thought would be good for traveling, then added to the pile some other essentials: a canteen for water, a small sleeping bag, a bit of rope (one could always use rope, she reasoned), and a small pouch of bandages.

When she was done, Kendra stepped back and stared at the pile. Something was missing.

"I wish I had some magic," she said to herself. In the stories she had read about great quests, the heroes always had some enchanted item to help them along, like a sword or a wand. But she had nothing of the sort.

Then Kendra remembered the magic carrots.

"That's it!" she exclaimed with a snap of her fingers. She reached into her pocket and pulled out five tiny seeds, all that were left from her morning's gardening experiment. Ratchet had given her the seeds a few weeks ago. But the carrots hadn't started growing until she was able to find the right incantation in Uncle Griffinskitch's *Gardening with Magic* book.

Kendra put the seeds into the bottom of her small belt pouch. She wasn't sure what use giant carrots would be on a long and dangerous journey, but they were the only magic items in her possession.

After a time, Uncle Griffinskitch came to check on her.

"Not a bad job," he murmured with grudging approval when he saw the belongings she had collected. "Now let's off to bed. We have an early start tomorrow."

Kendra didn't need to be told twice. It had been a long, adventure-filled day, and she was so tired that she thought she might fall asleep standing up. She crawled into bed and was soundly asleep before her long braids touched her pillow.

CHAPTER 8

Through the Magic Curtain

When Uncle Griffinskitch woke her, Kendra felt as if she had been asleep for only a few minutes. It was still so dark outside that she could see stars shining through her bedroom window.

"So early?" Kendra murmured groggily.

"Humph," her uncle muttered. "We need to be at the Elder Stone by dawn. And we're collecting Oki along the way."

After a hastily gobbled breakfast, Kendra and Uncle Griffinskitch locked up the house and set off down the path towards Oki's. The whiskery mouse and his family were awaiting them on the porch of their tiny home.

Oki's parents seemed to be in fine form, with his father saying such things as "Now you be careful" and "Put on a brave face," while his mother was working herself into a nervous frenzy about her son's upcoming adventure.

"Oh, it'll be horrible!" she exclaimed with gushing tears. "You'll contract Goojun pox or the squeezles! Or some Unger will eat you between pieces of toast for breakfast!"

"Oh, gee," Oki gulped.

"Or maybe you'll get squished by some giant!" Oki's mother wailed. "He could squeeze you until your eyes pop out of your head!"

"Humph," Uncle Griffinskitch muttered impatiently, as he ushered Oki off the porch. "I'm quite sure that won't happen. Now say your good-byes, Oki. The others are waiting."

Oki quickly waved his paw at his parents and tiny sisters and scampered off down the path, ahead of Uncle Griffinskitch and Kendra.

"Mother's been like that ever since she found out I was going on this darn quest," Oki said once Kendra had caught up to him. "I think she'll actually be disappointed if something doesn't happen to me!"

It wasn't long before they arrived at the Elder Stone, where Ratchet, Captain Jinx, and Professor Bumblebean were waiting for them. The professor looked as if he were on his way to study for some important exam, for he was carrying an enormous pack with books, scrolls, and maps poking out of every seam. As for Jinx, she looked to be marching into battle, for in addition to her trusty sword, she was strapped with all sorts of weapons: daggers, knives, and even a small axe.

"Well, we're all here now," Ratchet declared, waving them over to one of his jack-o'-lantern boats at the bank of the River

Wink. "Let's get a move on."

"I hope you picked a happy boat," Oki said to the raccoon. "If he starts yelling and cursing, he'll wake up the whole town."

"Don't worry about that," Ratchet assured the mouse. "I stayed up late last night making a special boat!" He pointed to the pumpkin, and Kendra could see that it had been carved with no mouth. The boat glared angrily at Ratchet, but of course, it was helpless to say anything.

"That will do the trick all right," Kendra said with a laugh, as she and the rest of the company boarded.

Once everyone was settled, Ratchet pushed off from shore, and they started down the river. Uncle Griffinskitch, Captain Jinx, and Professor Bumblebean chatted quietly about the task ahead. Kendra and Oki leaned over the edge of the pumpkin and watched the water go by. Ratchet concentrated on steering the boat.

They floated for over an hour in the darkness. Then, just

as the sun was beginning to peek its amber face over the horizon, they heard the roar of the mighty Wishing Falls, which spilled over a cliff at the very edge of Een. As the falls came into sight, Ratchet steered the boat ashore and brought it to rest on the bank.

"Well, here we are," Ratchet told his passengers. "Nothing between us and the outside world except the magic curtain."

Kendra found herself trembling, but she wasn't sure if it was from fear or excitement. She had never imagined she would go beyond the borders of Een, and now, here she was, only eleven years old and beginning a grand adventure.

"This is where we take leave of you, Ratchet," Uncle Griffinskitch announced, turning to the raccoon.

"I know, I know," Ratchet said.

"Good-bye, Ratchet," Kendra said, hugging the raccoon. "I wish you were coming."

"Now don't you worry—I'll be closer than you think," Ratchet told her with a wink. He patted Oki on the head, gave a nod to the others, and was soon on his way back down the river.

"Well, let's get going," Jinx said, pacing eagerly before the magic curtain.

Kendra nervously approached the curtain. She couldn't hear or see it, but she could certainly feel it. It was like a sheet of energy suspended in the air.

"Come on," Jinx said. "What's the holdup?"

"There's no way I'm going through that thing!" Oki declared. "I'll get zapped!"

"No, you won't," Jinx told the mouse. "Now march on."

But Oki wouldn't budge.

"If Oki's not going through, neither am I," Kendra announced.

"Maybe Elder Griffinskitch could put a spell on us," Oki suggested.

"What's that?" Uncle Griffinskitch asked.

"You know, to protect us . . . kind of," Oki stammered.

"Humph," Uncle Griffinskitch muttered, stroking his long white beard.

"I tell you what, Elder Griffinskitch," Jinx said. "I'll just throw each of these little twerps over a shoulder and carry them through myself."

"Humph," Uncle Griffinskitch grunted again. "Now listen, Kendra and Oki. The curtain is safe, I assure you. But it is still a magic thing. So you must concentrate very hard as you go through it."

"How do you mean?" Kendra asked.

"It's simple," her uncle replied. "Whatever you do as you cross through, don't think of onions."

"Onions!" Oki cried. "That doesn't make any sense at all."

Uncle Griffinskitch turned and glared down at the mouse. The old wizard's ears poked out from his white hair, burning red with anger.

"But I'm sure it'll work," the tiny mouse gulped.

"Now get on through," Uncle Griffinskitch commanded in his deep voice. "And remember: whatever you do . . . DON'T THINK OF ONIONS!"

Oki and Kendra turned and faced the curtain.

"Well, here goes nothing," Kendra said.

She took a deep breath, closed her eyes, and stepped through the curtain. She could feel her long braids buzzing with a crackle of energy, but it didn't hurt. Indeed, it felt as if the curtain were alive and tickling her. Then, just as suddenly, it was over, and she was standing safely on the other side. She turned and found Oki following close behind her.

"Don't think of onions, don't think of onions," the small mouse was murmuring, as if in some sort of trance.

"We made it through!" Kendra told Oki, shaking him to alertness.

"What a strange feeling," Oki remarked. "My whiskers are tingly."

"It's my braids that are feeling it," Kendra said, giving them a good tug.

The rest of the company was soon standing with them on the other side of the curtain.

"I don't get it," Oki said. "I know I wasn't supposed to think about onions, but in fact, that's the only thing I could think of!"

"You've been fooled," Jinx told him. "Old Griffinskitch just said that business about onions so you'd forget about how frightened you were."

"Is that true?" Kendra asked, turning to her uncle. The old wizard didn't reply, but Kendra couldn't help to notice a slight twinkle in his blue eyes. She had never known her uncle to play a trick of any sort before. She didn't even know he had a sense of humor. "How strange," she said to Oki.

"You know what's even stranger?" the mouse said. "Look back . . . I can't see Een anymore."

Kendra turned around and, sure enough, she could see nothing of the River Wink or anything else from home. The landscape seemed to just continue on as if Een didn't even exist.

"It's an illusion of course," Professor Bumblebean explained. "You see, the land of Een is invisible from the outside. Now you or I could march directly through the magic curtain and find ourselves home. But if a Goojun or some other monster were to blunder into the curtain, he'd just appear on the other side of Een without even knowing what had occurred."

"But if we can't see Een and we can't see the curtain, how will we find our way back?" Oki asked worriedly.

"You just have to know where you started from, of course," Professor Bumblebean replied. "Take a good look about you, Honest Oki, and mark the spot in your mind."

Neither Oki nor Kendra wanted to be stuck in the outside world. While the other members of the company consulted the professor's maps and did one last check of their supplies, the two young friends set about trying to memorize the landmarks around the curtain.

"We proceed due north," Professor Bumblebean declared shortly, pushing at his glasses. "We shall embark on a straight course towards those mountains. In those rocky pinnacles we will find our castle and—hopefully—the Box of Whispers."

CHAPTER 9

How Jinx Got Her Powers

The band of
would-be heroes
was now on its
way. Captain Jinx
took the lead, fol-
lowed by Kendra
and Oki, then
Professor Bumblebean, and
lastly, Uncle Griffinskitch, who shuffled
along with the help of his gnarled staff.

To Kendra, the world outside
the curtain seemed no different than the one
inside, though both
she and Oki expected
to find Goojuns and
Ungers around every
corner. Now, I'm sure
you'd be excited to
read about a Goojun
or an Unger, but Kendra
knew that even the thought of
such creatures was enough to send a shiver

down Oki's spine. Indeed, every time a leaf or branch brushed against his long tail, he jumped in the air and cried, "Eek!"

"Enough already!" Jinx snarled after Oki had jumped for the fourth time in less than an hour. "Why don't you just wave a flag and tell every monster from here to Krodos that we're on our way?"

"Oh, dear," Oki murmured. "Do you think they heard me?"

"Who?" Jinx asked crossly.

"Every monster from here to Krodos," Oki whispered.

"How should I know?" Jinx retorted. "Just try and keep quiet."

"Have you ever seen a monster?" Kendra asked the grasshopper.

"You sure are a talkative bunch," Jinx grumbled.

"Well, it helps pass the time, don't you think?" Kendra asked.

"Go talk to Bumblebore then," Jinx said, pointing to the professor, who was plodding a short distance behind them. "He likes to talk better than anyone I know."

"We'd much rather talk to you," Kendra told the captain.

"That's for sure," Oki agreed. "What do you think is in the Box of Whispers?"

"That's hardly my concern, or yours for that matter," Jinx replied. "Our job is to find it—and that's all."

"It must be important," Kendra said. "I mean, Elder Woodsong even called the orb to help find it."

"I think there are voices inside the box," Oki said.

"But whose voices?" Kendra wondered.

"Probably those of the ancient Eens," Oki replied. "That makes the most sense to me. But I don't know why they call it the Box of Whispers."

"Maybe the box isn't big enough to hold loud voices," Kendra suggested. "Maybe it can only fit quiet whispering ones."

"That's the silliest thing I've ever heard," Jinx declared.

"Well, what do you think then?" Kendra asked.

"I try not to think any more than I have to," Jinx retorted as they came upon a long branch lying across their path. If you had been the size of a grasshopper, the branch would have seemed like an enormous fallen tree. Still, Jinx was no ordinary grasshopper, and she threw the branch aside as if it had been no heavier than a feather.

Kendra and Oki looked at Jinx with amazement.

"How did you become so strong, Captain Jinx?" Kendra asked the grasshopper.

Jinx glared hard at the two young friends. "You are a pair of pestering twerps, you know that? Why should I tell you anything?"

"Please, Jinx?" Oki asked. "Tell us how you got so strong. I heard you drank a magic potion."

"I don't know how that's any of your business," Jinx scowled.

"Then tell us about the monsters you've seen," Kendra said.

"Who's said I've seen any?" Jinx demanded.

"Well, have you?" Kendra asked.

Jinx rolled her eyes. "Yes, of course," she said. "If you must know, I saw my first Goojun on the same day I got my strength."

"Really?" Oki asked. "Oh, do tell us about it."

"I'm no storyteller," Jinx grumbled.

"Please?" Kendra begged.

"I'll tell you what," Jinx said. "I'll cut you a deal. I'll tell you the story as long as Oki stops 'eeking.' And another thing! Don't go blabbing this to all of Eendom. That's all I need."

"Oh, we swear we won't tell," Kendra said.

"Double-swear," Oki added.

"You don't have to get dramatic about it," Jinx groaned, rolling her eyes at them. "Well, it happened long ago, when I was just a nymph. Don't ask me what that is, Kendra. That's what a young grasshopper is called. Anyway, I lived in the Hills of Wight, which are a good day's hop north of Faun's End. My parents had sent me there to apprentice with my Uncle Jasper, who was a great sorcerer."

"Greater than Uncle Griffinskitch?" Kendra asked.

"Well, I didn't say *that*," Jinx said, sounding annoyed. She took a deep breath and continued. "But he was a great wizard nonetheless. Sometimes Uncle Jasper would go outside the magic curtain to look for plants that he needed for all his powders and potions. He was a potion specialist, and Eens and animals came from every corner because he could heal all types of sicknesses."

"Oooh," Oki said. "Could your uncle cure Goojun pox? How about the squeezles?"

"Of course!" Jinx replied, though in truth she sounded somewhat uncertain. "Now stop interrupting, and let me continue! One day I went with Uncle Jasper to collect his plants. We went deep into the Forests of Wretch, for we were looking for this special kind of moss that only grows in pitch darkness. If any light touches this moss, it shrivels up and dies. But there's more than moss that lives in those woods."

"Like what?" Kendra asked, tugging nervously on her braids.

"Goojuns actually," Jinx said. "And that day we ran into a whole herd of them."

At the mention of Goojuns, Kendra looked at Oki and noticed a particularly strong "eek" welling up in him. But Jinx cast him a threatening glance, and at once, the mouse seemed to gulp down his terror.

"Uncle Jasper and I hopped for our lives," the grasshopper continued. "As I said, it was dark in the Forests of Wretch, and we got separated. Those Goojuns were everywhere. I couldn't yell for Uncle Jasper because I knew they'd hear me. So I made my way as best I could. I hadn't gone far when I stumbled upon Uncle Jasper's pouch. He kept all his potions in it."

"But where was your uncle?" Kendra asked.

"I don't know," Jinx replied with a grimace. "Since that day, he's never been seen."

"Oh," Kendra said sadly. "It sounds like what happened to my family."

"Well, I don't know much about that," Jinx said with some discomfort in her voice. "But the disappearances did happen in the same year. It wasn't long afterwards that Eens and we animals stopped going outside the curtain altogether."

"But how did you escape the Goojuns?" Oki asked.

"Like I said, I found Uncle Jasper's pouch," Jinx said. "And in it were all his potions. I could hear the Goojuns thrashing about in the forest. They were close to me, and I knew it would only be a matter of seconds before they caught me."

"Were you scared?" Oki asked intently.

"Well, the worst thing about Goojuns is that they don't eat you whole," Jinx said. "They like to eat you in little bits. They start with your legs, and then—"

"I do say," came a voice, and they looked up to see Professor Bumblebean. Having caught up to them, the large-eared Een had overheard the last part of Jinx's story. "Do you really think you should be describing such horrific scenes to these youths?"

"No less horrific then your giant swelled head, Boogerbrain," Jinx snarled.

"There's no need to be rude, Captain Jinx," Professor Bumblebean remarked. "And I do believe you have misspoken my name. It's Bumblebean, you know."

Jinx groaned.

"I should think you would recall the name Bumblebean," the professor continued. "After all, I descend from a long line of famous scholars."

"Oh, please finish your story, Captain Jinx," Kendra begged, interrupting the professor in her eagerness. She gave him an apologetic smile, then turned back to Jinx.

"I was just about to," Jinx told her, casting another sneer at the professor. "Anyway, *as I was saying*, I could hear the Goojuns getting closer. I began ripping through Uncle Jasper's pouch, for I knew he had a potion that would turn me invisible. But I was in such a hurry that I accidentally grabbed the wrong flask. Instead of an invisibility potion, I grabbed a healing potion, and I drank it down whole. Of course, I wasn't injured and didn't need to be healed. And because of that, the potion gave me super strength. To this day, it has never gone away."

"And the Goojuns?" Oki asked.

"They weren't much match for me after I took that potion," Jinx boasted. "I thumped them rather well, and sent them scampering back into the shadows of the forest. I looked for two days and nights for Uncle Jasper, but there was no sign of him. Finally, I went back home. But I never became a sorcerer. I was never that good at it to begin with, and once Uncle Jasper disappeared, I had no teacher. So instead, I studied the art of weapons."

"My word," Professor Bumblebean said. "Your story doesn't calculate, Captain. How on earth could you possibly select the wrong potion?"

"What do you mean?" Jinx growled.

"Well, I knew your Uncle Jasper," he declared. "He had an impeccable habit of labeling all his potions. Why didn't you just read the label?"

Jinx looked like she was about to explode in anger. "I told you," she roared. "I was in a hurry."

"Well, I do say, that's hardly an excuse not to stop and read," Professor Bumblebean said.

"You pompous, bungle-brained buffoon!" Jinx screeched. "Why don't you just mind your own business?"

"Well, I never!" the professor declared. "You don't have to lose your temper!"

With a furious scream, Jinx withdrew her sword and began slashing at the bushes and branches along the path. She was soon far ahead.

"Humph," Uncle Griffinskitch grumbled, hobbling up from behind. "What seems to be the problem, Professor?"

"I'm afraid I've provoked some agitation in the captain," Professor Bumblebean replied. "I'm not sure how, really. Nonetheless, it seems she's discovered a certain zeal for clearing the path."

"We don't exactly need the path cleared," Kendra said.

"Humph," Uncle Griffinskitch grunted in agreement, as he watched the grasshopper viciously swing her sword. "Just let her clear it all the same."

CHAPTER 10

An Uninvited Guest

The tiny band of adventurers traveled so late into the day that by the time they stopped to make camp, they were all quite tuckered out. Professor Bumblebean, who was not accustomed to exercise of any sort, seemed particularly exhausted. Kendra herself felt as if she had been in gym class all day without even stopping for recess.

Jinx would allow no fire, knowing that Ungers or Goojuns might see it in the night, so they had no warm meal. Instead, they nibbled on dried vegetables and fruit. Afterward, Jinx found some wild berries, so at least they were able to have what Oki called a "tolerable" dessert.

When the meal was finished, Professor Bumblebean promptly pulled out one of his books and began squinting at it through the moonlight.

"I do believe we are in the Hills of Horm," he remarked a short time later.

"Humph," Uncle Griffinskitch grunted. "Then we must be extra careful."

"Why?" Kendra asked. "What's in the Hills of Horm?"

"Oh, all varieties of monsters live here," Professor Bumblebean replied, too cheerfully for Kendra's liking. "More than I could enumerate. But this book states that, in particular, this is Unger territory."

"Oh, great," Oki fretted, looking about with worried eyes.

"You sure don't seem to be afraid, Professor," Kendra remarked.

"Oh, me?" Professor Bumblebean asked. "Well, fear is usually all just in our heads, I suppose. I choose to believe in facts over fiction. If only my fellow Eens would read more about these monsters, then I'm sure they'd be less afraid of them."

"Yeah, that'll work, Bumblesnore," Jinx said, sneering at the professor. "I'm sure that kind of knowledge would be really helpful while you're being gobbled down by some Krake."

"I do say," Professor Bumblebean said. "I'm afraid you must be quite addled, always forgetting my name. It's Bumblebean, you know. Perhaps if you had descended from a long line of scholars like myself, you'd have a better memory—or at least you might have cultivated a fondness for books."

"Why do I need books when I have you?" Jinx asked. "You're better than an encyclopedia, aren't you, Bumblebook?

Has that pile of paper told you anything useful yet?"

"My word, Captain," the professor uttered. "It's BUMBLEBEAN! And have you not heard a single word I just said?"

"Sure I did," Jinx replied. "You said we're surrounded by Ungers and all sorts of other monsters. Like we didn't know that already. We are beyond the magic curtain, after all."

"Well," Professor Bumblebean declared, "I'll have you know that this book also contains all sorts of information pertaining to the castle of Krodos, which, if you'll recall, is precisely where we're going."

"Who lives in the castle?" Kendra asked, crossing over to look at the professor's book.

"Giants, according to the records contained within this text," he replied happily.

"Does that mean it was a giant who stole the box?" Kendra asked.

"That can't be," Jinx said. "We'd have seen him."

"Not necessarily," Professor Bumblebean pointed out. "Whatever the species of this creature, it's certainly in possession of considerable magical ability. Remember, it was able to cross the curtain. So it certainly could have been a giant."

"Giants," Oki murmured, putting one paw to his forehead. "Why did it have to be giants? Why couldn't it have been something less . . . something less . . . well, something less giant?"

"Fear not, little one," Jinx said. "I reckon I'll just stroll up to one of those fellows and poke his eyes out!" With that, she withdrew her sword and began fencing with her long shadow in the cast of the moonlight.

"Heroic of you," Professor Bumblebean said. "If not somewhat reckless."

"Now listen here, you long-winded, dull-brained—," Jinx began.

"Silence!" Uncle Griffinskitch interrupted, putting a hand to his ear.

"What is it?" Jinx asked, brandishing her sword.

"I heard something," the old wizard said.

"I think it came from that direction," Professor Bumblebean said, pointing to a clump of nearby bushes.

Without a second thought, Jinx raised her sword and marched boldly into the brush.

"Where did she go?" Oki cried. "Is she all right?"

"Quiet," Uncle Griffinskitch warned.

Then suddenly, they heard Jinx shout, "Intruder!" and the bushes shook violently with the swinging of her sword.

"OUCH!" someone screamed, and a moment later Jinx reappeared with Ratchet staggering behind her. He was rubbing his sore bottom.

"You didn't have to jab so hard," he muttered, eyeing Jinx.

"Ratchet, what are you doing here?" Kendra exclaimed.

"As if I didn't know!" Uncle Griffinskitch boomed, his eyes flaring with rage. "I should have guessed that you couldn't leave well enough alone."

"Well, you might need me after all," Ratchet said in his defense. "You can't expect me to just stay behind."

"Humph," Uncle Griffinskitch snorted, and it was the type of angry humph that bordered on a "Days of Een!"

"I do say, your actions are immensely foolish," Professor Bumblebean lectured the raccoon. "Why, if the orb had wanted you to come, it would have—"

"Wait," Uncle Griffinskitch interjected suddenly.

"Now what?" Kendra asked, giving her braids a fretful tug.

"I heard something again," Uncle Griffinskitch said.

"Who else did you bring with you?" Jinx demanded of Ratchet.

"Why, no one!" Ratchet replied, crossing his arms angrily.

"Well, then what was it?" Jinx said. She raised her sword anxiously.

But before anyone could answer, the bushes ripped apart, and the tiny band of heroes found themselves face-to-face with a cluster of creatures so savage and so fierce that for a moment, everyone just froze. Kendra had never seen anything so frightening, not in her wildest imagination, not in her darkest nightmares. The beasts came out of the night all claws and fangs and grunts and snarls. No, she had never seen anything like them in all her short life. Indeed, she couldn't even say what they were.

But Oki seemed to know. "UNGERS!" he yelled, then—with a very loud "EEK!"—he turned and disappeared into the darkness.

CHAPTER 11

Kendra and the Unger

For once Kendra thought Oki wasn't overreacting. Even as the tiny mouse turned tail (and Professor Bumblebean wasn't far behind him), the largest of the Ungers raised a crooked club and smashed it into the dirt with such force that the whole ground shook.

"Days of Een!" Uncle Griffinskitch cried. "Get behind me, Kendra!"

Kendra's brain told her to listen to her uncle, but her legs were screaming at her to follow Oki. Now that the Ungers were upon her, they seemed even more frightening—if that were possible! They towered over Kendra like mountains, chiseled and hard, with skin as gray and rough as boulders, and arms like pillars. Coarse hair, as thick as wire, covered their backs, which were so humped that no shirt or cloak would fit them. Indeed, the Ungers seemed to wear no clothes at all other than ragged trousers. Even more hideous than their disfigured bodies were their heads. The savage creatures had small beady eyes set deep within their wrinkled faces and large yellow tusks that jutted out from wide crooked mouths.

It was no contest. Kendra's legs won out over her brain, and she turned and disappeared through the woods.

As she ran, she could hear Jinx yelling: "Meet the sword, you bloated bags of jelly!"

Kendra imagined the small and speedy captain leaping about the giant Ungers, jabbing them with her sharp weapons. Just knowing that Jinx was between her and the monsters made Kendra feel better—at least a little.

Kendra ran as hard as her legs would carry her. She was a good sprinter, and had won many races at school. But then, she had only raced against her classmates. It was a different story with a cluster of Ungers behind her. Kendra probably ran faster that night than she ever had before.

When she finally stopped, she realized that she was completely alone in the woods. There was no sign of Oki or Professor Bumblebean. She could only guess as to where they had run.

Kendra looked about her, but all seemed quiet. Then, a flash of bright light came through the woods, and Kendra heard an Unger let loose a mighty scream.

"Uncle Griffinskitch!" Kendra gasped, for she knew the flash had come from the old wizard's staff.

This brilliant light was quickly followed by the loud grunts of Ungers, for now the beasts came crashing through the woods as they tried to escape Uncle Griffinskitch's zaps of magic. Kendra perked her Een ears. The Ungers were coming straight her way!

Hopefully, you will be so lucky in life so as not to ever encounter an Unger stampede. If you do, it's strongly advised that you take cover, for some people say that a large horde of Ungers can trample an entire city to the ground quicker than you can say "flat as a pancake." A bomb shelter is often the best thing when it comes to Unger stampedes, but Kendra didn't happen to have one handy. So she found the next best thing—a small hole between the roots of a nearby tree. She quickly wriggled her way into the tiny hiding space. A second later, the stampede came. As the Ungers tore through the for-

est, Kendra could hear their howls and the snapping of trees. The ground trembled and clumps of dirt landed on her head as the giant monsters charged past. And then, just like that, they were gone.

Slowly and cautiously, Kendra poked her nose out of the hole and looked about. The night had gone quiet and still again.

"Well," Kendra said, still trembling from her near escape. "That was a close call. But I better find my way back to the campsite."

She set off through the woods. She hadn't gone very far when she heard a strange grunting noise that stopped her in her tracks. She gave her braids a nervous tug and listened again. Then she heard the grunt a second time. It was so quiet in the woods that the noise came clearly to her; and now she realized just how very close it was. Kendra inched towards the sound and soon found herself at the edge of a steep and rocky cliff. The grunt came yet again, and it was louder and closer.

Kendra peered over the jagged lip of the cliff. There, growling and moaning and clinging to the rocks for dear life, was an Unger.

Kendra jerked back from the cliff, her whole body shaking with fear. She could still hear the monster struggling against the rocks, its breathing hard and labored. What should she do? Part of her—a large part—wanted to run away. But the creature sounded as if it were in grave trouble. She had to look again. *It's okay,* she told herself. *You're safe. You're up here, and it's down there.* And she looked over the edge of the cliff once more.

It wasn't a very big Unger, she realized. Maybe it was just an infant. It still had tusks, but they were short and stubby, not long and curved like the others. Kendra stared hard at the beast. It wasn't that different from an animal, she decided. It had hair and claws, just like any other woodland creature. Compared to the other Ungers, it really was quite tiny, maybe only three or four times as big as her. Kendra looked past the Unger to the ground far below. If it were to fall, she knew it would die.

Then the Unger spotted Kendra. "Go awayzum!" he grunted. His voice was deep and threatening, but Kendra could see that his eyes were ablaze with fear.

"How did you end up hanging there?" Kendra asked, trembling as she spoke.

"Unger fleez Eeneez magic boltzum, tripzum, fallzum," the Unger snorted. "Other Ungers runzum away!"

"Just hang on," Kendra said, and now she could feel a tiny spark building inside of her, a spark that told her to take action. It was the type of spark that takes hold of you when you reach an important decision. Once that spark ignites inside of you, there is no way to extinguish it.

So it was with Kendra now. There was no time to think; she had to move fast. Frantically, she searched about the cliff edge, not exactly sure what she was looking for. There were lots of broken branches, but even if she could pass one down to the Unger, she was far too tiny to pull him up. She needed Jinx's strength, or Oki's cleverness, or Professor Bumblebean's intellect. Better yet, she needed Uncle Griffinskitch's magic.

"Magic!" Kendra exclaimed. She hurriedly reached into her pouch and pulled out the enchanted carrot seeds. "If this doesn't work, nothing will."

Kendra leaned out over the cliff edge and cast the seeds into the darkness, hoping that at least one of them would take root in the ground below.

"Whatzum Eeneez do?" the Unger demanded angrily.

"Just wait," Kendra replied. "Now all I need to do is to remember the right words."

"Wordzum?" the Unger asked anxiously. Kendra saw it was becoming more and more difficult for him to hang onto the cliff edge. At any moment, he was going to fall.

Kendra's memory kicked into gear. "I got them now!" She leaned as far over the cliff as she dared and chanted:

Humble seeds, cast to the earth,
Sprout to the clouds in glorious birth.
Tall and speedy, with mighty girth,
Vaster than an Eenling's mirth.

At first, nothing seemed to happen. Kendra listened hard, but the only thing she could hear was the desperate grunting of the Unger. Then, like a magic geyser of leaf and vegetable, a giant orange carrot emerged from the darkness beneath her.

"It's growing!" Kendra cried, as she watched the carrot rise from the rocky soil below. She chanted the spell again, over and over, prompting the enchanted vegetable to grow faster and taller.

"It's going to come right past you," Kendra called to the Unger. "Grab on to it as it goes by."

The Unger's eyes were wide and frightened. Kendra could see that the strange carrot terrified him. But the creature had no choice; if he didn't take her help, he would plunge to his death. With a gnarled claw, the small Unger reached out and seized the leafy top of the carrot. Wrapping his muscular legs around the stem, he hung on for all he was worth. Only a few seconds later, the carrot reached the top of the cliff. The beast scrambled onto the ground alongside Kendra and lay there, panting heavily.

"Whyzum Eeneez helpzum Trooogul?" the Unger demanded, after it had caught its breath.

"Is that you?" Kendra asked. "Trooogul?"

"Yeezum," the Unger replied, his voice deep and gravelly.

"I'm Kendra," the Een girl said.

"Whyzum helpzum Trooogul?" the Unger repeated.

"I . . . I don't know," Kendra admitted. Suddenly, she started trembling again. Only a moment ago, she had been elated at the success of the Unger's rescue. Now fear had overtaken her, and she could barely speak.

"Eeneez no helpzum Ungers," Trooogul declared. "Itzum forbidden! Youza getzum expelled frum Eenzum! Foreverzum! Everyonezum knowzum—evenzum Trooogul!"

Kendra gasped. How could she forget about the sacred Een code? How could she forget that helping an Unger would mean being kicked out of the land of Een forever? Kendra looked hard at Trooogul. But then again, how could she have let him fall to his death? Kendra's mind was racing.

Then, suddenly, she heard Uncle Griffinskitch's voice.

"Kendra! Where are you?" the old wizard called from the ragged forest.

Kendra cocked her ear to the voice then turned to look back at Trooogul. "What now? Are you going to hurt me?"

"Unger no hatzum Eeneez," Trooogul snorted. "Youzum! Youzum no likum Unger. Eeneez come to Unger place! Youza trespazzum!"

"I-I'm sorry," Kendra stuttered.

"Nowzum youzum leave!" Trooogul barked. "Leavezum beforezum Unger angrezum more!"

Kendra nodded and turned to go.

"Waitzum!" Trooogul rumbled.

A shiver went down Kendra's back. She turned and found herself face-to-face with the Unger. He was so close that she could see his eyes gleam in the moonlight. She could feel his hot breath on her face. For a minute, he said nothing, and the only sound in the night was his harsh gasping.

"Unger thankzum little Eeneez," Trooogul grunted.

Then, before Kendra could reply, the great beast turned and bolted into the darkness, leaving her to wander back through the woods alone, towards the sound of Uncle Griffinskitch's voice.

CHAPTER 12

A Night's Shelter

"There you are!" Uncle Griffinskitch boomed as Kendra came into sight. "I've been looking all over for you. I told you to stay with me."

"I-I-I was scared," Kendra stammered.

"Humph," he muttered, and it was the type of humph that Kendra couldn't even begin to decipher. Her uncle's face was pale, his eyes wide with fright.

But what is he afraid of? Kendra thought to herself. *Uncle Griffinskitch is no typical Een. I can't imagine him being afraid of any Unger!*

"Come now," the old wizard said gruffly, as he turned and led

Kendra back toward the campsite. "You're safe now. Captain Jinx and I were able to scatter those beasts."

"What did you do to them?" Kendra asked, as she followed after him.

"Not as much as I wanted to," Uncle Griffinskitch grunted. "Unfortunately, they all escaped."

"Oh," Kendra said, looking worriedly at him. *How can I tell him about Trooogul?* she asked herself. *I can't. He won't understand. He sits on the council; he'll just have me exiled. I can't tell him. I can't tell anyone.*

And now you know, reader, the secret that I spoke of at the very beginning of this tale. Kendra forged it at that very moment, vowing to tell no one about how she had saved the life of an Unger.

Of course a secret—a really important one—can be a heavy burden to bear, and Kendra began to worry about it almost immediately. It weighed so heavily on her that she didn't even realize that she and her uncle had arrived back in camp until Oki came charging up to her.

"Kendra!" the tiny mouse cried. "You're all right!"

"Yes," Kendra said weakly. "What happened to you?"

"I found him and the professor stuck in a bramble bush," Jinx said. "Isn't that right, Bramblebean? How did your books and facts help you in the face of an Unger? And Oki was just chanting over and over again 'Don't think of onions, don't think of onions!' As if that would help against an Unger."

"I thought it might make me forget how scared I was," Oki informed Kendra.

"Did it work?"

"No," Oki confessed, "but thinking about onions is better than thinking about Ungers."

"Kendra, you scared the wits out of me by running off like that," Ratchet said.

"Never mind what you think!" Jinx scolded. "You have no right to even be here, Ratchet."

"Precisely," Uncle Griffinskitch said. "It's only the first day of the quest, and you've nearly ruined everything."

"Ah, don't be so dramatic," Ratchet muttered. "Those Ungers would have happened upon you no matter what."

"Is that so?" Uncle Griffinskitch demanded, banging his staff against the ground. "And tell me, Ratchet Ringtail, what do you know about the world beyond the magic curtain?"

"Yeesh," Ratchet said. "I'm sorry, okay? There, I said it. I'll go back home as soon as morning comes."

"Humph," Uncle Griffinskitch snorted. "I'm afraid, Ratchet, that you'll be going back sooner than that. And this time, I will take an extra measure to make sure you don't follow us again."

"What does that mean?" the raccoon asked nervously.

"Humph," the old wizard grunted again. "Just a little

spell. It shouldn't hurt too much." He waved his gnarled staff at Ratchet and, in his very deep voice, proclaimed:

Tiny bell, loud and clear,
Sounder than an Eenling's fear,
Whenever you find Kendra near,
Shake and shudder for Eens to hear.

There was a sharp flash of light and a cloud of smoke. When the haze cleared, Kendra could see that Ratchet was now wearing a tight collar around his neck. A large bell was hanging from it, and it rang loudly.

"As long as you're in earshot of Kendra, that bell will sound," Uncle Griffinskitch informed the raccoon. "So follow us if you like, Ratchet, but now I'll know. And next time, I will not be so kind."

"Turn this thing off!" Ratchet cried, tugging at the collar. "It's darn annoying!"

"The only way to turn it off is for you to get as far away from Kendra as soon as possible," the old Een wizard said.

"But Uncle Griffinskitch!" Kendra exclaimed. "Can't you at least let him spend the night? You're not going to make him go home in the dark, are you?"

"We're all going to have to travel in the dark," Jinx announced, gathering up their packs, which were still scattered about from the Unger attack. "We can't stay here any longer. Those Ungers could come back with more of their pals. I'm afraid there will be no sleep for any of us tonight!"

"Well, Ratchet Ringtail?" Uncle Griffinskitch asked, eyeing the raccoon. "Have I made myself clear?"

"Yes!" Ratchet replied, pulling desperately at the collar.

"Humph," Uncle Griffinskitch said. He waved his staff again at the raccoon and muttered another incantation. "Now get that ringed tail of yours back to Een as fast as you can. And mind yourself! I don't need to be rescuing you from some two-headed giant or other such nonsense."

"I'll be careful," Ratchet promised.

"Come now," Jinx urged the rest of the company. "Let's get a move on."

"Bye, Ratchet," Kendra called meekly to her friend as she picked up her pack and dusted it off.

"Bye, Kendra," Ratchet called back. "Be careful!"

Kendra set off through the woods behind Captain Jinx and the others. She could still hear Ratchet's bell ringing. It wasn't until a few minutes later that it finally fell silent.

"Well, that settles that," Uncle Griffinskitch muttered.

On through the night, the tiny company marched. Kendra was exhausted. Each and every step took so much effort that it felt as if she was walking through quicksand. The sun stretched its arms of light upon a cold and dreary day, and still, they walked on.

"When can we stop?" Oki asked over and over again. "Aren't we far enough away from the Ungers yet?"

"I'll let you know when, so you can stop asking," Captain Jinx told the mouse. "The farther we get, the better."

And so they continued on through the rest of the day. The landscape grew more rugged and more tangled, and with each step the tiny band of travelers grew more tired.

At last, as the second evening approached, Jinx stopped in front of an old hollow log.

"We'll stop here," she declared, after inspecting the fallen tree to make sure it was safe. As the rest of the company climbed wearily inside, Jinx drew her sword and assumed post at the open end of the log.

"What are you doing, Jinx?" Kendra asked. "Aren't you going to sleep?"

"No, I'll keep watch," the grasshopper replied. "We can't all go drifting off. It's too dangerous."

"Look at Uncle Griffinskitch," Kendra said. "He must be exhausted."

The old Een had wandered to the very back of the log, collapsing into a heap of white hair. The curls of his whiskers

fluttered up and down as he lightly snored.

"And no wonder," Professor Bumblebean said. "He has been toiling harder than anyone."

"What do you mean?" Kendra asked.

"His magic has played a large role in sheltering us from the dangers of this outside world," the professor explained. "He's been exerting all his strength to create a magic shield to hide us from the prying eyes and sniffing noses of the Ungers and other creatures that so like to catch us."

"So that's why Ratchet got us into such trouble," Kendra said. "Uncle Griffinskitch's spell wasn't cast over him because he didn't know he was there! So even though those Ungers couldn't see or smell us, they probably sniffed Ratchet out. And, of course, he led them straight to us."

"The whole quest was nearly thwarted because of his reckless actions," Professor Bumblebean said. "Pursuing us was a selfish decision."

"He was just trying to help," Kendra said defensively.

"He didn't appreciate the consequences of his actions," Professor Bumblebean said. "The outside world is a dangerous place, and one that is not to be taken lightly."

"But now Ratchet's alone," Kendra said, unable to let the matter rest. "He still doesn't have Uncle Griffinskitch's spells to protect him."

"Not to worry," Professor Bumblebean said. "I saw your uncle flash his staff slyly over that raccoon just before he sent him on his way. He delivered him with enough of a shield to get him back home. But it consumes a great deal of energy to use so much magic. I suspect he hasn't used that much power in years."

"Let him sleep through the night," Jinx said from her post. "We'll need more of his magic stuff yet before this journey's out."

"For once we are in agreement, Captain," Professor Bumblebean told her. "Now, Oki and Kendra, it's off to bed for us."

As they unrolled their sleeping gear, Kendra ventured a question that was weighing very heavily on her mind. "Professor, why is it forbidden for Eens and monsters to, er . . . help each other? What would be so bad about it? Helping a Goojun or Unger, I mean."

"What are you talking about, young one?" the professor asked. "The monsters that inhabit the outside world are the sworn enemies of all Eens. Why would anyone want to help them?"

"Well, I thought maybe we could all just get along?" Kendra suggested meekly.

"Get along!" Professor Bumblebean exclaimed. "We can't get along with the monsters of the outside world! Look at what just happened! They tried to kill us! What are you thinking, Kendra? That they would have you over to dinner? Maybe they'd have you for dinner, that's all I know! I do say!"

"Okay," Kendra said nervously as she crawled into her sleeping bag.

She couldn't help thinking about Trooogul. He certainly hadn't tried to eat her. He had told her that he didn't hate Eens. But could she believe him? *What's wrong with me?* Kendra wondered. *Ungers are the enemies of my people, and any normal Een would have just let him fall. But how could I have just left him there to die? He needed my help. He would have died. Still, he is an Unger,* Kendra sighed. Her mind was whirling. *Everyone's always said it, and now I've proven it,* she told herself. *I'm just not a normal Een.*

CHAPTER 13
The Shrieking Skarm

For how long she slept, Kendra did not know, but her dreams were not peaceful ones. She dreamt she was walking through a meadow near her house when she heard a whisper from behind her. At first she could not make out what the voice was saying in that foggy dream world, but then she felt a tap on her shoulder and turned to find herself surrounded by the Council of Elders. "Een has helped Unger!" they cried all together, pointing at her. "Een has helped Unger!"

Then a violent shriek broke across her dream, so loud and frightening that it reminded Kendra of the sound the dark shadow had made when it stole the Box of Whispers. She looked up into the sky, but it was blue and empty. Then, the scream came again, ripping across her mind with such ferocity that she bolted awake.

Have you ever awoken suddenly to discover what you thought you were hearing in your dream was not a dream at all? That's exactly what happened to Kendra. The shrieks hadn't come from inside her head—but from the real world.

"What is that?" she cried. She scrambled out of her sleeping bag, her braids brushing the top of the log in which they slept.

The other members of the company were also now awake, their eyes all turned towards Jinx, who was still standing watch at the edge of their shelter.

"Some sort of monster," the grasshopper reported, clenching three different weapons among her various hands. "But don't ask me what kind—I don't know."

Kendra and Oki poked their noses out the end of the log and looked to the faint, early morning sky. There was more shrieking, so loud and sharp that they rubbed their ears.

"Look! There it is!" Oki cried, pointing to the clouds. "It's a flying worm!"

Kendra couldn't have described the monster better. It had a short fat body that tapered into a long tail, and a pair of spiny wings that cast a dark shadow upon the ground. The worm's skin was thin and green with brown blotches, and it had only two tiny legs that ended with hooked claws. A single round eye darted about on its head (indeed, it seemed as if the eye *was* its head), while a long, sharp tongue zipped in and out of its fang-encrusted mouth.

"My word!" Professor Bumblebean uttered as he joined the others at the end of the log. "It's a skarm."

"A what?" Jinx asked.

"A skarm," the professor repeated, quickly flipping open his *Comparative Book of Creatures*. He read: "Skarm live in scattered forests and meadows, and are nocturnal by nature. In a group they are known as a senate. Their diet consists of—"

"Oh, do shut it, Bumblebrag," Jinx muttered.

"You must be overcome with fear to be forgetting my name again," the professor told Jinx. "How many times have I told you? My name is BUMBLEBEAN."

Jinx was about to muster a reply when Oki suddenly let out a sharp, "Eek!"

Everyone looked upward again. The skarm had suddenly turned and was now flying steeply towards the hollow log.

"It knows we're here!" Oki whispered hoarsely.

"Everyone to the back," Jinx ordered, herding the group to the rear of the log. She had no sooner spoken than they heard a loud thump, and the log took a sudden lurch, throwing them to the ground.

"What's going on?" Kendra cried.

"The skarm has landed on top of the log," Uncle Griffinskitch said. Now they could hear the slithering creature as its claws rasped across the wood above their heads.

"Don't think of onions, don't think of onions," Oki murmured frantically.

"Quiet!" Jinx hissed, clutching her sword tightly. "We have to get out of here!"

But at that moment, the opening of the hollow log was darkened with the giant peering head of the skarm. As soon as

it spotted the company, it released a dreadful shriek and sent its tongue flickering towards them.

"We're trapped!" Professor Bumblebean cried. Now that the skarm was right on top of him, it seemed the professor had forgotten his scientific curiosity, for he was trembling as hard as Oki.

"I'm going to lure this overgrown slug out of here," Jinx declared, slashing at the skarm's tongue with her sword. "Elder Griffinskitch, you get everyone else out."

"Hold on a minute, Captain," Uncle Griffinskitch said. "We may be able to fight our way past this creature."

"No way," Jinx retorted abruptly. "You've had a lot of magic knocked out of you the past couple of days, Elder Griffinskitch. Trust me. I'll take care of the one-eyed freak, and you get the rest of our gang to safety. Don't worry. I'll catch up with you later."

Jinx didn't wait for further argument. She used her strong hind legs to bound past the skarm and out of the log and into the open. With a scream, the skarm tore after her.

"Hurry!" Uncle Griffinskitch commanded the remaining members of the company. "Let's go!"

They scrambled out of the log and darted into the underbrush of the woods. The skarm was still shrieking and the small band of companions could not help but to turn and gaze back upon Jinx. The bold grasshopper was fiercely swinging her weapons, lunging forward at the skarm even as the hideous creature attacked with its long, sharp tongue. Jinx dealt the worm-like beast a mighty blow of her sword, and at once, the skarm went squealing into the sky. Jinx turned and hopped quickly back to them.

But the skarm wasn't finished. It turned in the sky and winged back towards Jinx, its claws extended.

"Watch out!" Kendra shouted.

Jinx didn't have a chance to react. The skarm scooped her up with a violent screech and, quicker than a blink of its single bloodshot eye, returned to the sky. Jinx was gone.

CHAPTER 14

M Into the arshlands

Kendra was stunned. One minute Jinx had been there. The next she was snatched up in the claws of the skarm.

"She's dead and gone!" Oki wailed.

"Humph," Uncle Griffinskitch muttered. "We don't know that."

"I do say, Elder Griffinskitch, what should we do now?" Professor Bumblebean asked.

"There's nothing we can do but go on," the old wizard replied.

"But we can't just leave!" Kendra cried. "We have to try to save her."

"There's nothing we can do," Uncle Griffinskitch said, a soft sadness in his voice. "How can we chase the skarm? That dreaded creature is across the skies now."

"But—"

"Kendra," Uncle Griffinskitch said, cutting her off. "Let's trust that she can look after herself. It is Jinx, after all. In any case, she made a brave sacrifice so that we can continue our search for the Box of Whispers. And that's what we must do. Now, come on."

So, with heavy hearts, the remaining members of the company fell into line after Uncle Griffinskitch, and they left behind the hollow log and the site of Jinx's heroic last stand.

They traveled hard for the next few weeks, stopping only to sleep, eat, and take the odd short rest. The mountains drew ever closer, looming like a row of jagged black fangs. Much to Kendra's despair, there was no sign of Captain Jinx. Uncle Griffinskitch tried to encourage her to keep hope for the tough little grasshopper, but Kendra held less and less with each passing day.

In addition to the sadness she felt for Jinx, Kendra continued to struggle with her nightmares. Each and every night, she found herself immersed in a horrific dreamworld plagued by never-ending chants of judgment: "Een has helped Unger! Een has helped Unger!" Sometimes it was Uncle Griffinskitch who spoke the words, sometimes other members of the council. Sometimes it was no one at all, and the words just hung over her head like a dark thundercloud, ready to rain down punishment on her. And yet, no matter whose voice it was, it always sounded the same: dark and venomous and cold.

Kendra woke each morning thoroughly terrified. If she were found out, she would be cast from Een, left to wander the outside world forever. She shivered at the very thought. If Jinx, so strong and brave, could not survive the outside world, how could she? Kendra had never felt so helpless and alone. She could not tell anyone her secret, yet the secret itself gnawed at her like a monster, hungry and relentless.

The only thing that compared to the fright of Kendra's nightmares was the landscape itself. You have probably never been near the mountains of Krodos, but let me tell you—they are a wretched, wild place. With each passing day, the way became more tangled, more ominous. The very ground was now damp and soggy, and the air had turned so hazy and thick that they couldn't even see the sun.

"Marshlands," Uncle Griffinskitch said grimly.

"Well, our proximity to Krodos is increasing then," Professor Bumblebean remarked. "My maps tell me that once we cross the marshlands, we'll be near the foot of the mountains, where the castle rests."

The journey through the marshlands only became tougher. The ground was muddy and thick, and long brown reeds stretched above their heads. The swamp had a sharp pungent smell that stung Kendra's nostrils. With no sun or moon, time had little meaning. Kendra was not sure how her uncle knew when to stop and rest, or when to continue. She had no idea. She felt as if the fog were choking her, and she was chilled right to the bone. Sometimes, she felt as if she would never be warm again, no matter how tightly she wrapped her cloak around her frigid body.

As Kendra plodded through the thick mud, hour after dreary hour, her mind began to fill with all sorts of strange thoughts. There was, of course, the voice from her dreams that continued to haunt her. On top of that, she began to imagine she would find her mother amidst the foggy ghost world of the swamp. Any second, she thought her mother would just magically appear and say, "Why, Kendra, there you are! I've been waiting here all these years for you. Let me take you and your friends out of this wretched swamp."

It was all in her mind, of course, but Kendra began seeing all sorts of strange shapes in the fog. Finally, on what her uncle said was the third day in the marsh, Kendra saw the tiny figure of Captain Jinx standing before her.

My mind is playing tricks on me again, Kendra told herself.

"I told you'd I'd catch up with you," Jinx declared.

"Except you're not even real," Kendra sulked.

Jinx laughed and, with a mighty leap, landed in the soft earth right in front of Kendra, spraying her with mud.

"Captain Jinx!" Kendra cried. "It is you!"

The rest of the company gathered about the grass-hopper, their faces beaming with smiles. Kendra and Oki

were so happy they wanted to hug Jinx, but the feisty grasshopper warded them off with a dangerous wave of her sword.

"None of that mushy stuff!" she warned.

"But Captain, how did you survive?" Kendra asked.

"That pesky worm tried to feed me to its babies," Jinx explained. "But I gave it a piece of my sword, I'll tell you that! Once it was tuckered out, I took a piece of rope from my pack and harnessed that foul slug so that I could ride it into the marsh and look for you. I jumped off its back two days ago and have been looking for you ever since."

"Welcome back, Captain," Uncle Griffinskitch said warmly.

"You have made a remarkable escape," Professor Bumblebean told Jinx. "However, I can't help but wonder if you haven't traded one misfortune for another."

"What are you talking about, Bumblehead?" Jinx snorted.

"Why, I believe your encounter with the skarm has dam-

aged your brain," the professor said. "The name is Bumblebean, remember? And what I mean is that we've been wandering around here for days."

"Well, I'm here now," Jinx declared. "I'll get us out of here."

She assumed the lead of the company, and with a lighter spirit, they set off through the marsh again. But after several hours, it appeared they were still going about in circles.

"Well, my mother never guessed that I would die in a fog," Oki said.

"Oh, you're always in a fog," Jinx retorted crossly.

"I do believe I will consult my maps," Professor Bumblebean declared.

"You egghead," Jinx said. "Your maps aren't exactly going to part an opening through this wretched fog, are they?"

"Well . . . no," he admitted.

"Uncle Griffinskitch, don't you have a spell to help us?" Kendra asked.

"Humph," the old Een grunted. "I can make a light shine from my staff, but a light certainly won't help us in this haze. It'll just bounce back at us."

No one knew what else to say. They were all exhausted, so they just stood there, in the fog on the wet ground, waiting for something to happen. And then, something *did* happen. And that something was a voice, traveling towards them across the marshlands, soft and distant.

"I say, whatever could that be?" Professor Bumblebean

asked, cupping a hand to one of his large, pointed ears.

"Shhh," Jinx said, listening hard.

They all listened. Then, quite distinctly, they heard a song through the fog:

> *Gold, gold,*
> *Beautiful gold.*
> *The most wondrous thing*
> *I ever know'd!*

This was followed by a long string of giggles that sounded rather like "tee hees." Kendra and the rest of the company looked at each other blankly, not sure what to make of the strange voice. It came again:

> *Gold, gold,*
> *Beautiful gold.*
> *The most wondrous thing*
> *I ever know'd!*

"It's no monster, that's for sure," Jinx said excitedly. "It could even be an Een!"

"Whoever it is, he has atrocious grammar," the professor announced.

"Who cares, Bumblebutt?" Jinx retorted. "We could use a friend right about now. Let's go!"

"I'll lead the way this time, Captain," Uncle Griffinskitch declared, hobbling over to the front of the group.

Jinx opened her mouth to argue the point, but the grizzled Een was already shuffling through the fog, and it was either follow or be left behind.

CHAPTER 15

They Meet
Pugglemud

Quickly,

the companions trudged through the marsh, following the sound of the strange voice. Whenever the voice stopped, Uncle Griffinskitch stopped, for it was the only thing that provided them with direction. The voice continued to sing and giggle, growing louder and louder until, at last, they saw a light burning through the fog.

"It's a campfire!" the professor said excitedly.

"Eh?" came the voice through the fog. "Who goes there?"

"It's I, Gregor Griffinskitch, from

the land of Een," the wizard replied, staggering ahead. "My company and I have lost our way in the marsh."

Kendra and the others hurried after Uncle Griffinskitch. They soon found themselves in a small clearing, amidst a messy campsite where a large, Een-like creature sat on an overturned pot.

"A Dwarf!" Jinx exclaimed.

Kendra had never seen a Dwarf. He was more than twice the size of an Een, but he had similar features. His nose was long and sharp, and he had two large ears that narrowed at the ends. The hair on his head was as red as his beard, which sprouted out from his face in a tangled mess of twigs and leaves. Mischief danced in his twinkling eyes, and when he smiled, Kendra could see two crooked rows of rotting teeth. He had a round belly that stretched the buttons on his patched and ragged coat, which, like everything else in the camp, was streaked with grease and dirt.

"What's this?" the Dwarf said, rising to his small wiry legs to inspect his visitors. "What d'ya call yerselves now?"

"We're Eens," Professor Bumblebean announced. "Except for the mouse and grasshopper, of course. But I can assure you that they are true allies."

"Never heard of 'em," the Dwarf said. "Eens that is."

"My word!" Professor Bumblebean exclaimed. "How could you have never heard of the marvelous land of Een?"

"Ya got gold there in that land of yers?" the Dwarf asked.

"Why, but a little," the professor replied.

"A little?" the Dwarf said. "Well, I don't care too much fer a land that has but a little gold!"

"And from where do you hail exactly?" Professor Bumblebean asked, seeming somewhat appalled by the stranger's talk.

"Where most o' my kind comes from, of course," the Dwarf replied. "From Umbor."

"Ah," Professor Bumblebean said. "The vast underground kingdom of the Dwarves."

"That's right," the Dwarf said. "Now tell me, who you folks be?"

Uncle Griffinskitch introduced each of them by name. "And you?" the old wizard asked when he was done.

"I'm Pugglemud," the Dwarf replied.

"Is that your first or last name?" Professor Bumblebean asked.

"Jus' Pugglemud to you folks," Pugglemud said. "No self-respectin' Dwarf tells strangers his whole name. Now what do you funny critters mean by comin' into my camp?"

Kendra looked about and wondered how Pugglemud could even call it a camp. If you have ever let your room go without tidying for more than a few weeks, then you might be able to picture what the Dwarf's camp looked like. Cans of food—some open, some half-empty—were strewn about, spilling their innards over Pugglemud's clothes and other possessions. There was a small tent (which was really nothing more than a blanket thrown over an arched branch), along with a variety of pots, kettles, and other strange tools. A small rusty cauldron simmered on a fire, emitting a less than pleasant smell.

"We can't get through the marsh," Jinx told Pugglemud. "Do you know the way out?"

"I might," Pugglemud said, eyeing Jinx and her vast assortment of weapons. "Now where might you be headed fer?"

"To Krodos," Uncle Griffinskitch replied.

"Krodos!" Pugglemud exclaimed. "Well, I'll not be takin' you there, that's fer sure!"

"I do say! Why not?" Professor Bumblebean asked.

"Cuz you'll just be stealin' my gold," Pugglemud accused.

"Gold!" the professor cried. "What gold? I see no gold here."

"That's cuz I don't have it yet, don't ya know," Pugglemud replied. "But I will. It's a waitin' fer me in the castle. Tee hee!"

Uncle Griffinskitch and Professor Bumblebean exchanged quizzical glances. "You're going to Krodos?" Uncle Griffinskitch asked. "And there's gold there?"

"As if you didn't know, Mr. Sneaky Long-Hair!" Pugglemud said, pointing a scraggly finger at the wizard. "Piles o' gold. Chests bustin' their guts with gold. It lines the floor like a carpet! Tee hee!"

"Now look here," Professor Bumblebean said. "We're not goldseekers or treasure hunters. We want nothing to do with the gold . . . even if it is yours, which, I suspect, it is not!"

"Are you callin' me a thief?" Pugglemud demanded.

"No, of course he's not," Uncle Griffinskitch said, somewhat impatiently.

"Well, where d'ya think them giants got it all from?" Pugglemud asked.

"They stole it, that's a where! From every corner of the known earth, don't ya know! So what's wrong with stealin' from a thief?"

"What you do at Krodos is your business," Uncle Griffinskitch told Pugglemud sternly. "We have our own treasure to find there."

"Treasure?" Pugglemud said, his ears noticeably perking up.

"*Not* gold," the wizard grunted. "Let's just say it's a . . . personal item. Nothing that a fine Dwarf such as yourself would ever want to trouble with."

"Well, it's of no account anyhoo," Pugglemud told them. "I still ain't takin' you to Krodos. Why would I?"

"We may be of use to you," Jinx offered.

Kendra watched Pugglemud cast a critical eye at the grasshopper. "You?" he said. "A tiny whelp of a thing such as yerself? What help can you offer?"

"How'd you like to find out about my 'help'?" Jinx asked, her hand reaching for her sword.

"There's no need for that, Captain," Uncle Griffinskitch said, casting a critical eye at Jinx. "Nonetheless, she is right, Pugglemud. We can be of assistance. We have magic and maps, which we would be willing to share with you. As long as you can get us out of the marsh."

"Magic, eh?" the Dwarf said, sitting back down on the pot that served as his makeshift chair. "You be a wizard then?"

Uncle Griffinskitch nodded in reply.

"How do I know yer tellin' the truth?" Pugglemud asked.

"Humph," Uncle Griffinskitch snorted. "I assure you, I am a wizard."

"Well, I think ya better give me a bit of a demonstration," Pugglemud said.

"Humph," Uncle Griffinskitch snorted again, and Kendra could tell that it was the type of humph that meant he was losing patience. She knew her uncle wouldn't want to waste his magic. But then again, he had to convince the Dwarf to help them. The old Een closed his eyes and began waving his staff in the air.

"Ain't nothin' happening," Pugglemud declared, still planted firmly on his overturned pot.

"I do say," Professor Bumblebean said, "you must give it a moment."

"Give what a moment?" Pugglemud demanded. He stirred uncomfortably, for it seemed that his seat—the pot—was suddenly becoming warm. In fact, it was becoming more than warm; the whole pot began to turn red and hiss with steam.

"Yikes!" Pugglemud cried. He leapt to his feet, and now, all could see that his trousers were on fire. "Put me out! Put me out!" he screeched, slapping at the flames shooting out from his bottom.

Jinx was more than happy to oblige him. With a dirty skillet that was lying on the ground, she scooped up some marsh water and doused the Dwarf.

"There you go," she said as Pugglemud glared down at his smoldering bottom. "Convinced yet?"

"Think yer funny, don't you folks?" Pugglemud said irritably. "You just wrecked my best pair o' trousers."

"Gee, I'd hate to see his worst pair," Oki whispered to Kendra.

Uncle Griffinskitch waved his staff again, and Pugglemud's trousers were magically repaired. Indeed, Kendra thought they now looked in better condition than before the demonstration. "Now," Uncle Griffinskitch said to Pugglemud. "Let's discuss an arrangement to get out of this swamp."

Pugglemud rubbed his bushy red beard and for the longest time didn't say a word. Uncle Griffinskitch and the rest stood there uncomfortably until at last the Dwarf spoke: "Well, I got my own magic stuff. Still, I ain't no wizard. And they say there's fierce beasts guarding all that gold fer them giants. Are ya sure yer not after my gold?"

"Absolutely not," Uncle Griffinskitch said.

"All right then," the greasy Dwarf said. "But if ya cross me, there'll be trouble."

"You can trust us," Uncle Griffinskitch promised.

"Then we have a deal," Pugglemud said, sticking out his hand to shake with the wizard. "I'll help you get outta the swamp, and you'll help me get to all that gold. Tee hee! Now let's sit down and eat somethin' before we get on our way."

With that, the ragged Dwarf bent over his campfire and gave his dinner pot a cheerful stir. Whatever he was cooking smelled horrible, and Kendra couldn't help but to wriggle her nose in disgust.

"The thing is," Kendra heard Captain Jinx whisper to Uncle Griffinskitch, "can we trust him?"

CHAPTER 16

Oki Gets into Trouble

Sometimes,

a little hope can go a long way. Just knowing that the marshlands would soon be behind them lifted the hearts of the company. They happily ate their meal, and afterwards, Pugglemud packed his camp. (Though Kendra noticed that he more or less just crammed everything into one large knapsack.)

"So, how do we get out of here?" Captain Jinx asked the Dwarf.

"Eh? Oh, that's not so tough," Pugglemud said, pulling out a small silver cylinder. It looked rather like a flashlight, but when he flicked the switch, it didn't cast light, but instead a perfect window through the fog. For the first time in days, they could suddenly see into the distance.

"My word!" Professor Bumblebean exclaimed. "What an incredible device!"

"Like I said, I have some of my own magic," Pugglemud said.

Kendra and the others fell in line behind the Dwarf and set on their way. Their pace was now quick and sure, and only a few hours later, they left behind the marshlands and reentered a world of light and sunshine.

"Myself, I don't like no sun," Pugglemud said, squinting. "We Dwarves are used to bein' underground huntin' fer gold and such. That swamp suited me jus' fine. But the castle of Krodos ain't in that marsh, so we gotta leave it behind."

"The mountains are closer than ever," Jinx said, pointing to the cold blue peaks that towered before them. "We still have a few hours of light left. I bet we can reach them before nightfall."

"A good plan," Professor Bumblebean agreed. "Let's put as much distance as possible between us and that swamp."

Kendra was glad to feel the warmth of the sun on her head again. The dampness and gloom had been adding to her mood of fright and despair. For a moment, at least, she felt a little better. They marched hard, without break, and it wasn't long before Oki started complaining to Kendra that he had to go to the bathroom worse than anytime he could ever remember.

"You better ask Jinx if we can stop," Kendra told him.

"No way!" Oki said. "She's grouchier than ever since being stuck in that marsh."

"I'll ask her then," Kendra said. "Jinx, can we stop? Oki needs a bathroom break."

"Why didn't you go back in the marsh?" Jinx demanded of Oki.

"I didn't have to go then," Oki replied. "But I really have to go now."

"I want to make the mountains by nightfall," Jinx said over her shoulder. "We're not stopping now. Just hold it."

"But—"

"You can always go and catch up with us afterwards," the grasshopper said flatly.

"I'll wait for you, Oki," Kendra told her friend.

"No, then we'll both be left behind," Oki said. "I guess I'll just try and hold it."

Of course, this was easier said than done. If you have ever been on a long car ride without knowing when the next bathroom was going to appear, then you probably know exactly how Oki felt. Kendra did her best to distract the little mouse, but it seemed he could think of nothing but going to the bathroom.

Finally, they reached the base of the mountains, and Jinx stopped so they could set up camp. Oki eagerly dropped his pack and darted for the bushes.

"That's a strange little feller," Pugglemud said, as Oki scurried past him.

"You don't know the half of it," Jinx muttered.

When Oki returned to camp, he was trembling head to tail. This didn't really surprise Kendra, for most everything seemed to put a fright into Oki, but what did startle her was that his whole body seemed to be changing color.

"Oki!" Kendra cried, taking a close look at the mouse. "What happened? You're turning yellow!"

"What do you mean?" Oki asked, but when he held his paws up, they were indeed turning yellow.

"And your tail!" Jinx exclaimed, bounding over to the mouse. "It's yellow, too!"

"What?" Oki cried, frantically twirling around, trying to see his tail.

"What's going on now?" Uncle Griffinskitch demanded, for now Oki had captured the attention of everyone in the camp.

"All I did was go to the bathroom," Oki told the old wizard. "But there was this big flower, and it got upset."

"How does a flower get upset?" Jinx asked impatiently. "Flowers don't talk."

"This one does," Oki said uncomfortably. Not only was he turning more yellow with each passing moment, but his body was beginning to swell up like a balloon.

"My word!" Professor Bumblebean declared, and he hurriedly began flipping through one of his books.

"Well, what did this plant say?" Kendra prodded Oki.

"It was a real grouch," he said. "Grouchier than . . . than . . . than . . ."

"Grouchier than what?" Kendra asked.

"Well, grouchier than Jinx," Oki said.

"I'll show you grouchy," the grasshopper snarled, but now Oki was beginning to swell so much that he was growing in size. He now easily dwarfed Jinx.

"We have to do something!" Kendra cried. "What's happening to him?"

"Where is this plant?" Jinx demanded, craning his neck to look at Oki's changing form. "I'm going to have a look."

"No!" Uncle Griffinskitch commanded. "It's obviously dangerous. Quickly, Oki, tell us what else happened."

"Well, as I was going to the bathroom, the plant started yelling at me," Oki explained. "It said, 'How would you like it if I went into your house and just started peeing everywhere?' And all I could think of was how upset my mother would be if anyone started doing that, let alone some strange plant, and—"

"Get to the point," Uncle Griffinskitch grunted. Oki was growing more round and bulbous with each passing moment, and they all had to step back to keep out of his way.

"I think you critters are more trouble than yer worth!" Pugglemud remarked. "I never heard of no strange plants 'round here."

"Well, this one is strange," Oki squeaked. "It coughed on me!"

"Did you say 'cough'?" Professor Bumblebean asked,

but before Oki could answer, he threw down his book and began flipping through another.

Long green stalks were now beginning to grow out of Oki's ears and the top of his head, and giant tears began rolling down his cheeks.

"There's no reason to cry," Jinx told him. "We'll find a way to fix you."

"That's not it," Oki said. "My eyes are stinging so much that I can't help crying."

"Stinging!" Kendra cried. "I don't get it."

"Don't worry," Professor Bumblebean said, "I've read about this plant. It changes you into whatever you are thinking about when it coughs on you. This is very interesting!"

"Not to me!" Oki cried.

"Oh, no," Kendra groaned. "Oki, just what were you thinking of when that plant coughed?"

"Days of Een!" Uncle Griffinskitch cried, as he gazed up at the giant round bulb that was now overtaking the mouse's entire body. "Onions!"

"You idiot!" Jinx snapped at Oki. "Always thinking about onions."

"Well, technically speaking, I'm sure he was trying *not* to think about onions," Professor Bumblebean said.

"Oh, my," Oki murmured. "I don't think I'll ever go to the bathroom again!"

"Well, ya gotta," Pugglemud said, trying to console the mouse. "You just can't go turnin' off them waterworks, don't ya know!"

"Waterworks?" Oki said. His feet had completely disappeared, and now he rocked back and forth on the round bottom bulb of the onion plant that he was becoming.

"Myself, I only go once a day," the Dwarf announced. "But I pass a lot of wind, so maybe that makes up fer it."

"This isn't helping," Oki fretted, but it was becoming harder and harder for him to speak, for his mouth was disappearing.

"It's beans that give me the worst gas," Pugglemud continued. "Whew! You don't want to be around me after a plate o' good beans!"

"I hardly want to be around you at all," Jinx snapped.

"Oh, please everyone, stop arguing so that the professor can find a cure for Oki!" Kendra cried.

"Ah, here it is!" Professor Bumblebean declared, pounding his fist on his open book. "It's called the wheezing wonder plant of Krodos. Its scientific name is—"

"Oh, do hurry, Professor," Kendra said. "Isn't there some way to help Oki?"

"Of course," the studious Een replied, pushing up his glasses. "There's an antidote to this unfortunate condition our dear Oki has contracted. Let's see . . . oh, Elder Griffinskitch, I'll need your help to collect some ingredients. Then we need to boil up a small potion."

"But how will Oki drink it?" Kendra asked worriedly.

"Well, we spray it on him," the professor replied. "Rather like fertilizer, I do think."

Uncle Griffinskitch peered into Professor Bumblebean's book and began memorizing the list of ingredients.

"I've got it," he said after a moment. The old wizard turned and quickly hobbled out of sight.

"Oh, look at him now!" Kendra exclaimed, for now Oki could not be recognized at all. He had completely transformed into a giant onion.

"He must have been thinking about a pretty big onion," Jinx remarked.

"Or *not* thinking about one," Professor Bumblebean added.

It was only an hour or so later when Uncle Griffinskitch returned with a small sack full of strange flowers and grasses. "Let's get a pot boiling," he said. "We'll have to risk a fire for once. I'll do my best to shield us from any monsters that might be out there."

"I wouldn't be worrying about that anyhoo," Pugglemud said as Kendra and Jinx began gathering up a small pile of sticks for the fire.

"Why do you say that?" Professor Bumblebean asked.

"Because this ain't the friendliest part of the world, don't ya know," Pugglemud replied. "Even Ungers and fellers like them know enough to stay away . . . less they mean to go rob the castle like us folks."

"Well, despite your intentions, we certainly aren't here to rob or plunder," the professor declared.

"Sure, whatever you say," Pugglemud responded.

"Just how much gold do these giants have, anyway?" Professor Bumblebean inquired.

"Beats me," Pugglemud said. "All I ever heard is rumors. I never actually met anyone who went to the castle and lived to tell about it!"

It took twenty minutes for the cauldron and its belly of ingredients to come to a boil, another hour for it to simmer, and yet another for it to cool. It was an anxious time for Kendra, but at least it helped take her mind off her own troubles.

The sun had completely set by the time Professor Bumblebean and Uncle Griffinskitch finally took the potion and poured it into a small pouch. Jinx used one of her tiniest knives to poke a line of holes in the bottom of the pouch. And there they had it—a homemade watering can.

Uncle Griffinskitch waved his staff, and the bag magically floated above the large onion that had once been Oki, sprinkling potion on the plant's long green stalks. In only a few minutes, these stalks began to wither and retreat, the bulb of the onion started to shrink, and soon enough, Oki was standing before them, good as new.

"Oh, thank goodness you're okay," Kendra told her friend, hugging him tight.

"My mom was so sure that something horrible would happen to me," Oki said, clearly relieved to be back to his normal self. "But I bet you she never imagined that I would have been turned into an onion!"

"There you have it, Captain," Professor Bumblebean said to Jinx. "My books have proved their usefulness after all."

"It's true," Jinx said. "I even used some of your pages to start the fire."

"What?" the professor cried, but Jinx was only joking.

"Humph," Uncle Griffinskitch grunted. "This has been enough excitement for one day. Everyone to bed. Tomorrow, we venture into the mountains."

CHAPTER 17

In the
Footsteps
of
Giants

The sun had
barely peeked over
the horizon when the
company awoke the next
morning. They hurriedly broke
camp and set forth into the
mountains. After an hour or so,
they arrived at a wide crevice that
cut the mountainside in two.

"I've never seen such a strange
canyon," Jinx remarked.

"That's because this ain't no
canyon," Pugglemud said. "It's
a path."

"A path!" Professor Bumblebean
exclaimed. "My word! It's gargantuan."

"Well, it was made by giants,
don't ya know," the Dwarf said.
"They hacked a road right through
the mountain. This here path
should lead us right to the back
door of the castle."

"Oh, my," Oki fretted. "Maybe I'll

just stay here and guard the entrance to the mountains and make sure no one follows you in."

"Make sure you don't think of onions then," Jinx said. "That way you won't notice the giants when they come up behind you."

"On second thought, I'll just stick with you guys," Oki said quickly.

Without further discussion, they entered the mountain crevice and began their way up the rough and rugged path. The cliffs on either side rose sharply above them, casting them in shadow. Soon, they were all huffing and puffing, for the path was so steep that in some places it felt as if they were climbing rather than walking.

About midday they turned the corner and came face-to-face with a gigantic axe, lying haphazardly against one side of the mountain pass. The menacing weapon looked as if it had been there for hundreds of years. Its wooden handle had mostly rotted away while its blade was dented and streaked with rust. Next to the axe was a clutter of strange objects: bent and twisted shapes of yellow. Some were black and charred as if they had been scorched by fire. There was also what seemed to Kendra to be an immense boulder, though it was also yellow, and strangely round on top.

"Let me guess," Jinx said, gazing upon the huge axe with an envious glint in her eye. "This must have belonged to a giant."

"W-w-we must be drawing closer to the castle, I suppose," Professor Bumblebean declared, stammering with fear in spite of himself.

"But what are all these other strange objects?" Kendra

asked, looking at the yellow shapes. "They look like logs. But then where are the trees?"

"There ain't no trees because they ain't logs," Pugglemud declared. "They're bones! The bones of a giant. And see, that big boulder-like thing? That's what's left o' his skull."

"Oh, my word!" Professor Bumblebean gasped, finding himself a seat on a rock.

But Oki did the opposite of sitting. At the mention of a giant, he let out the loudest "EEK" of his life, then turned tail and ran down the path, back from where they had come.

"Captain!" Uncle Griffinskitch shouted. "Stop him!"

But Jinx was already on her way. With one mighty leap, she landed on top of the frightened mouse and threw him to the ground.

"Shut it!" she cried, clamping a hand over Oki's mouth. "Do you want the whole castle to know we're here?"

Oki quieted down. Jinx pulled the mouse to his feet and brought him back to the group.

"They're jus' bones, don't ya know," Pugglemud told Oki. "This feller here has been dead a long time by the looks o' it."

"He certainly didn't perish from natural circumstances," Professor Bumblebean remarked, wiping his forehead with a handkerchief. "He must have been compromised in some dreadful conflict."

"Humph," Uncle Griffinskitch muttered, and Kendra knew it was the type of humph that meant he was eager to move on. "Let's go," he ordered.

Oki looked so terrified that he could barely move his legs. Kendra took his little paw, hoping to calm him, but she nearly had to drag him past the skeleton and up the path.

They had gone only a short distance farther when the castle of Krodos came into view. Even after witnessing the skeleton, the castle was bigger than Kendra could have ever imagined, a colossal collection of towers and turrets that rose ominously out of the craggy cliffs to block out the sun.

"I do say," Professor Bumblebean murmured. "The pictures in *The Illustrated History of Krodos* simply don't do the real thing justice. This castle is . . . is . . ."

"I don't believe it," Jinx said with astonishment. "Are you actually at a loss for words, Blabberbean? I've been waiting for this day for weeks."

As they drew closer, they were able to get a better view of the castle. There was no questioning that the fortress had once been the site of some grisly battle, for the stones were battered and streaked with thick black soot. Some of the higher walls were punctured with holes.

"This castle is a mess," Kendra remarked.

"She looks like a pretty face that's been punched in the nose, that's a what," Pugglemud added.

"How are we supposed to get inside?" Kendra asked.

They could see an immense door set in the side of the castle, but it was as tall as a tree. There was no way they could even begin to think of opening it, even if it weren't locked (which they were sure it was). Jinx thought they should be able to squeeze underneath the door, but it was the type of gate that was pulled from the top, so there was not a sliver of space available.

"Can ya open it with yer magic?" Pugglemud asked Uncle Griffinskitch.

"Not in a way that won't wake every giant in Krodos," the old Een replied.

"Now what?" Kendra asked.

Then suddenly Jinx gave a whoop. "Look here!" she called. "I've found a way in."

CHAPTER 18

Professor Bumblebean and the Riddle Door

Have you ever looked all over for something, only to finally find it sitting right in front of your face, in the most obvious place? Well, that's exactly what happened with our heroes at the gates of Krodos. They had been looking for a giant door, when in fact the whole time there was a normal-sized door right in front of them. They had simply overlooked it, for it was made from the same stone as the rest of the castle wall and had no visible markings. In fact, it didn't even have any handles.

"How strange," Jinx said. "Why would giants have such a small door?"

"I reckon they got theirselves Goojun slaves and such," Pugglemud said. "Those poor fellers would need a way in and out too, don't ya know."

139

"Humph," Uncle Griffinskitch grunted. "Their misfortune, but some luck for us."

"Let's get inside," Pugglemud said. "On the other side of this here door is all that wonderful gold . . . tee hee!"

Captain Jinx pushed on the door, but it would not budge.

"Now what?" Oki asked.

"Perhaps I can find a password that will open the door," Professor Bumblebean mused, opening up his pack of books.

"Never mind those books, Bumbleweenie," Jinx said, drawing her sword. "I'll see if I can pry it open." She slid her weapon into the thin crack of the door and pried it with all her might.

"Ouch!" the door suddenly cried, so surprising Jinx that she leapt backwards.

"That voice came from the door!" Professor Bumblebean cried in astonishment.

"Of course it did!" the door exclaimed, and now they could see a pair of eyes and a large mouth magically appearing in the rock face. "You'd scream too if someone stuck you with a sharp sword!"

"Well, if I had known you could feel it, I wouldn't have done it," Jinx grumbled, acting somewhat angry that the door had scared her so.

"Oh, great," Oki murmured. "I'm getting rather tired of things talking that normally should not."

"Hey? What's that?" the door asked.

"Nothing," Uncle Griffinskitch said, stepping before the door. "We mean to pass."

"Well, you won't be doing that unless you can solve my riddle," the door said.

"We had no idea you were a riddle door," Jinx grumbled. "You could be a lot less difficult, you know."

"And you could be a lot less dangerous with that sword," the riddle door retorted.

"Enough!" Uncle Griffinskitch said impatiently. "Please, then—give us your riddle."

"Very well," the door said. "Now, let's see . . ." It rolled its large black eyes, as if deep in thought. "Once there was . . . no, no . . . I used that one last time. Hmm, how about . . . oh, no, no . . . that will be far too easy!"

"Get on with it!" Jinx griped. "We haven't all day."

"Oh, all right then," the door muttered. "I get so few visitors. You could stand to be a bit more polite, you know. Nonetheless, here is your riddle: There is an Unger who lives on the other side of the marsh, in the boot of a giant. Seven children she has. Exactly half of them are boys. How can this be?"

"That's an impossible question!" Kendra cried. "Half of seven is three-and-a-half. And you can't have half an Unger, can you, professor?"

"Of course not," Professor Bumblebean replied firmly.

"Well, this is your folks' type o' business," Pugglemud said. "I ain't no good at these little word games. I got you fellers outta the marsh, so now you get me through this darn door."

"We'll solve it, not to worry," Professor Bumblebean assured the Dwarf.

"Maybe one of the children is really small," Kendra suggested. She couldn't help thinking of Trooogul. He hadn't been all that small, but she supposed baby Ungers might be.

"You can't count an Unger as half just because it's small," Oki said.

"Give up yet?" the riddle door asked with a mischievous chuckle.

"Of course not," Jinx said. "We just need a bit more time."

"There is no answer!" Oki cried in frustration. "The door just doesn't want us to get in."

"Oh, I assure you, there is an answer," the door declared.

Uncle Griffinskitch stroked his beard thoughtfully. "Humph," he muttered. "Let's review the facts. The Unger has seven children in total."

"Don't forget—she lives in a boot," Oki added.

"That hardly matters," Jinx told the mouse.

"Well, it must be a big boot after all," Oki said.

"Does she cook onions in there?" Jinx teased the mouse.

"Silence!" Uncle Griffinskitch snorted. "Concentrate on the facts of the riddle."

"Well," Professor Bumblebean said, "We know there are seven Ungers. Half of them are boys."

"Then what are the other half?" Kendra asked. "If half are boys, then the other half must be girls."

"Of course, you only get one guess," the riddle door said. "If you guess wrongly, then I'm afraid you've missed your chance."

Professor Bumblebean sighed and scratched his head. "Well, we must be particularly careful then," he said. He made himself a seat out of a pile of his books and sat down on it so that he could think extra hard.

It seemed to take him a long time. The door sighed with impatience from time to time, and Kendra tugged on her braids out of nervousness. Then, suddenly, the

professor burst to his feet, his eyes afire with excitement. "I do say!" he exclaimed. "I've got the answer: they're all boys! And that, Mr. Door, is your answer. Exactly half of the Ungers are boys because they are *all* boys!"

"Good job, Professor," Uncle Griffinskitch said. "The riddle is solved."

The riddle door sighed again. "Indeed, it is," it said, the disappointment clear in its voice. "Therefore, you may pass."

With a long, moaning creak, the door swung slowly inward, revealing a passageway that stretched away into darkness. Jinx peered into the tunnel and gulped so loudly that Kendra heard it. Then with a wave of her sword, Jinx led the way inside. As soon as the last of them passed through, the riddle door closed behind them with a loud "click" and an even louder chuckle, and the company suddenly found themselves in pitch darkness.

Jinx whirled around. "I didn't like the sound of that chuckle," she said, fumbling in her pack.

Kendra couldn't see Jinx, but she could hear her rustling. "What are you looking for?" she asked the grasshopper.

"This," Jinx said, producing a small torch, which she lit and held to the closed riddle door. "Hello!" she called. But there was no response.

"What seems to be the dilemma, Captain?" Professor Bumblebean asked worriedly.

"Look," Jinx replied. "There's no handle, no face, no door."

"Where did it go?" Oki asked nervously.

"Nowhere," Uncle Griffinskitch replied. "It's a riddle door. You can only see it from the other side because it only goes one way."

"What's that mean?" Pugglemud asked.

"It means we're not getting out of here the way we came in," Jinx said grimly.

CHAPTER 19
The Vault of Riches

When

you have no way back, then you just have to keep going forward, and that's exactly what the group had to do. The passageway, like everything else in the castle, was simply enormous, and Kendra felt tinier than ever. When anyone whispered, the voice echoed in the darkness. No one dared to speak too loudly. The passage was like the darkest, most uncomfortable basement you can imagine, the type that is cold and dank—even on the hottest summer day. As usual, Jinx led the way, holding a torch in one hand and her sword in another. The passage was so quiet that Kendra could hear Oki gulping and murmuring about onions. It only added to her own nervousness, and she was just about to ask him to be quiet when Jinx came to a sudden stop. Kendra bumped right into her.

"Careful," Jinx whispered.

"What is it, Captain?" Uncle Griffinskitch said, shuffling up from the rear.

"I thought I saw someone looking at me," Jinx explained. "But look. It's just an eye painted on the stone. The entire wall is one giant mural."

She held her torch close to the wall so they could all see. The painting was so big and the light so dim that it was hard to get a sense of it. But they could all clearly see the eye that had surprised Jinx. It was part of an enormous picture of a dragon. It was so life-like that Kendra had to keep telling herself that it was just a painting. The mural stretched down the entire wall for as far as she could see, and it showed every scale and detail. It was a deep orange color, which caught the light of Jinx's torch and made it look even more realistic.

"Why, look," Professor Bumblebean said. "The whole corridor is adorned with paintings."

They walked ahead and gazed in wonder upon the artwork along the passageway. The murals depicted all sorts of strange and hideous creatures: dragons, Ungers, and some that they couldn't even identify.

"This place gives me the creeps," Oki declared.

"For once I agree with you," Jinx said. "Let's move on."

They plunged ahead into the darkness, eager to leave the frightening paintings behind. They took many twists and turns. To Kendra it seemed as if the journey would never end. Then, at last, they turned a corner and saw a light shining from what looked to be the end of the passage. As they crept further up the hall, the light became so bright that Jinx extinguished her torch. She led the company into the light. Soon they were standing on a wide balcony. Kendra hurried over to the railing and found herself looking upon a palatial room with a high vaulted ceiling. But it wasn't the ceiling that was so incredible, it was the floor, sparkling as bright as the sun.

"Treasure!" Kendra gasped, rubbing her eyes in disbelief.

The rest of the company rushed to the railing.

"Not jus' treasure!" Pugglemud exclaimed excitedly. "GOLD!"

"Come on!" Jinx called, waving them over to the far side of the balcony. "There's a staircase here."

Pugglemud was halfway down the stairs before the grasshopper even finished her sentence. It was slower going for Kendra and her companions; the stairs had been built for giants, of course, and it was not an easy descent for their tiny legs.

"Hey!" Jinx called after Pugglemud. "What about some help?"

But Pugglemud didn't seem to hear her. He tore down the rest of the stairs and dove headfirst into the mounds of treasure. "Gold!" he cried, tossing the coins into the air so that they came back down and bounced off his head. (Though if they hurt, he hardly seemed to notice.) He began swimming through the piles of gold as if he were some sort of strange fish, giggling the whole while.

"Figures," Jinx muttered, as she and her companions struggled down the remaining stairs.

After a few minutes, they reached the floor. If the vault had seemed spectacular to Kendra from above, it was even more so now that she stood amidst the sea of glittering wealth. To her, it seemed as if the giant chamber contained all the treasure in the world. The room was simply bursting with riches. And it wasn't just gold, for there were other prizes too: shimmering mirrors, sparkling scepters, polished swords, hand-carved vases, gleaming goblets, casks of brilliant diamonds, and gems colored red, green, and blue. Then Kendra noticed something that no one else had yet seen: one small box, dark and purple and winking with yellow stars. It was sitting by itself on a pedestal, in the very center of the room.

"The Box of Whispers!" Kendra gasped, and the rest of the company all turned at the sound of her voice.

Kendra, of course, had never seen the magic chest before—but there was no mistaking it. Strange, magical, and mysterious, the box almost seemed alive as it radiated a soft halo of light and throbbed ever so gently on its quiet perch, as if it were struggling to contain thousands of voices harbored deep within its core. And, straining her pointed ears, Kendra could almost hear the voices, almost—but they only came across as muffled whispers, as if she were trying to listen to them from around a dark corner or behind a closed door.

Then Kendra noticed the key. It was long and gold, and it was hanging from a small hook on the pedestal. She remembered what the elders had said. It would be disastrous if the box were opened. But part of her couldn't help imagining what it would be like to thrust the key into the lock and reveal its mysterious contents.

Then her thoughts were interrupted by the sound of Uncle Griffinskitch's deep voice.

"Thank goodness!" he muttered. "The box is safe."

It seemed as if everyone let out a collective sigh of relief. After weeks of travel, they had finally found their prize.

"In one way, I can't believe how easily we discovered it," Professor Bumblebean remarked after a moment.

"It was almost too easy, if you ask me," Jinx said. "No giants, no guards. There's nothing protecting the box except that darn riddle door and a pile of bones."

"Humph," Uncle Griffinskitch muttered, and Kendra couldn't help but think that it was the type of humph that meant he agreed with Jinx. She looked over her shoulder, half-expecting giants to suddenly appear. But the only sign of activity in the chamber came from Pugglemud, who was still gleefully frolicking in the treasure.

"I'm starting to get the creeps again," Oki squeaked.

"Did you ever stop?" Jinx retorted anxiously.

"Well, I suppose we should be happy with so quickly finding the box," Professor Bumblebean declared. "After all, our mission has been a success."

"Let's not congratulate ourselves quite yet," Uncle Griffinskitch said. "We still have to find a way out of here. Let's make haste."

"Do you want me to take the box?" Jinx asked.

"No," the old wizard replied. "It's better for you to keep your weapons at the ready. Oki, you can carry the key, and Kendra, you take the box."

"Me?" Kendra gasped. She couldn't believe that her uncle would entrust her with such a responsibility. He usually seemed so disappointed with her, but now he was asking her to carry the fabled box of whispers.

"You can do it," Uncle Griffinskitch said. "These are magic things, but they won't hurt you. I promise."

Oki took this as his cue and lifted the key from its hook. It was so long that when he held it upright, it was taller than him, but it was light enough for him to carry.

"I'm ready," he announced.

All that was left was the box. Kendra stared at it, anxiously tugging her braids.

"Quickly," Uncle Griffinskitch said. "Here, I'll carry your pack for you."

Wordlessly, Kendra handed her pack to her uncle and stretched her hand towards the box. It seemed to shudder as she touched it, and for a moment, she drew her hand back.

"Hurry!" Uncle Griffinskitch urged.

Quickly Kendra removed the enchanted chest from its pedestal. As she cradled the box within her arms, it seemed to throb with life, beating like a heart, as if it were alive. *What is in this thing?* Kendra asked herself as she tried to contain the box's mysterious energy.

"C'mon!" Jinx urged. "Let's get out of here."

"What should we do about him?" Oki asked, pointing to Pugglemud. The Dwarf was so entranced by the piles of gold that he was completely oblivious to their presence.

"He won't even know we're gone," Jinx said. "We've got our treasure; he's got his. I'd say everyone's happy."

"I wonder which way is the best to take our exit," Professor Bumblebean wondered aloud.

"There's no sense going back up those stairs," Jinx said. "That'll just lead us back to a dead end."

"There's only one other way out of this vault," Uncle Griffinskitch said, "and that's through the front door."

They scrambled across the treasure towards the massive door that stood at the far side of the room. It was slightly ajar, and gold coins spilled through to the passageway beyond.

"Well, here's our way out," Jinx said, sliding through the crack.

The others followed. They now found themselves in a passageway that looked much like the one that had led them to the vault in the first place. They forged ahead. Beads of sweat rolled down Kendra's face, and she realized that the passage had grown suddenly hot. She felt like she could barely breathe, but there was nothing to do but stumble ahead into the eerie blackness.

"Look, here are more paintings," Professor Bumblebean announced, pointing to the passage wall. "These giants possess certain artistic ability. Why, look at this dragon. This painting demonstrates such technique and realistic style."

"Cut the chatter, Babblebean," Jinx whispered over her shoulder.

They tiptoed past the dragon painting, and the box pulsed strongly in Kendra's hands. It was almost as if it were trying to escape from her. Kendra gazed up at the towering wall of fire-red scales as she walked past what seemed to be the dragon's long snout. The painting seemed so real. Though it was

dark, she could see the outline of each scale. She could see the dragon's nostrils. She looked way up and saw where the giants had given the beast a gigantic, closed eyelid.

"This must be exactly what a real dragon looks like," Kendra murmured quietly.

Then, suddenly, the enormous eye opened.

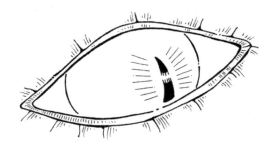

CHAPTER 20

Uncle Griffinskitch Fights the Beast

Kendra

stopped dead in her tracks, frozen with fear.

Oki, whose eyes were mostly squeezed shut, walked right into her.

"Ouch!" he cried. "Kendra, what are you doing?" Then he followed her gaze to see the giant blinking eye of the dragon.

"EEK!" Oki screeched.

"Quiet!" Jinx scolded. "What's gotten into you?"

"Dr-dr-dr," Oki stuttered.

"What?" Uncle Griffinskitch asked gruffly.

"Dr-dr-dr," Oki stammered again, now shaking uncontrollably.

Kendra herself couldn't find her voice at all. The box was now glowing brightly in her hands. She could feel it pulsate against her body.

"My word!" Professor Bumblebean cried impatiently. "Speak, little one."

"Dr-dr-dr-DRAGON!" Oki finally cried, pointing upwards.

Everyone now looked up, just as the gargantuan dragon seemingly came alive and rose to his full height. Kendra could not have dreamed of a bigger, more ferocious creature. He was covered in thick red scales that clattered and clicked with the rippling of his muscles. Two long leathery wings were folded in sharp angles upon his back, though Kendra could not imagine how he could fly in the narrow passages of the castle. As for his claws, these were sharp and gnarled, and he had a long tapered tail that thrashed about the passage like a whip. Inside his mouth were rows of tiny, sharp teeth that dripped with rancid green saliva, and out of the back of his throat flickered a tongue so long and slithering that it reminded Kendra of a snake. And, of course, there were his eyes, large and yellow and gleaming like mirrors.

It was with these eyes that the dragon now gazed upon Kendra and her friends. Then, without warning, the monster unleashed a dreadful shriek, a sound so loud and piercing that at once everyone stumbled backwards. It was a shriek they had all heard before—on the very day the box had been stolen.

"Days of Een!" Uncle Griffinskitch exclaimed. "The Red Thief!"

"WHO DARES TO STEAL THE BOX OF WHISPERS?" the dragon bellowed. "For I am Rumor the Red Dragon, keeper of all treasures known to man or monster, and that box is my most prized possession!"

The dragon's voice was so loud that it seemed to reverberate through the entire castle. Kendra gasped and her eyes went as wide as two full moons. She had heard Rumor's voice before—

in her dreams—a hundred times over the past days and weeks. As she stood before the dragon, a cold chill going down her spine, Kendra realized that it had been his voice all along: "Een has helped Unger! Een has helped Unger!" Now, the nightmare was real. She was facing her accuser. But how could it be? Her mind began to swirl with questions, but only for a moment. Jinx grabbed her by the arm and swung her about.

"RUN!" the tiny grasshopper yelled.

Kendra clutched the Box of Whispers and fled down the passage until she reached an enormous door. She had no choice but to stop. "What now, Captain Jinx?" she cried.

But there was no reply.

"Captain Jinx?" she asked, turning around. Uncle Griffinskitch, Professor Bumblebean, and Oki were at her side, panting from their run. But there was no Jinx.

"Where did she go?" Kendra asked, desperation in her voice.

"There!" Oki cried, pointing back down the passageway.

Kendra looked down the dark hall, but could see nothing but the giant dragon. Then she caught a glint of metal. It was Jinx, standing before the mighty beast, her tiny sword drawn in proud defiance. With the immense monster looming over her, she looked smaller than ever. But this didn't seem to stop her. She rushed forward, slashing at the dragon's giant toes, but the instant she struck the tough, armored scales, her sword snapped in half like a twig.

Rumor let out a loud laugh, and the whole passage seemed to tremble. Then, he drew back and unleashed a jet of flames upon the passage.

"Uh-oh! Not good!" Jinx cried, squeezing her eyes shut.

But the flames never reached her. Before Kendra could realize what was happening, she saw Uncle Griffinskitch, with his magic staff, standing in front of Jinx. He had turned the fire into a shower of flower petals that now floated harmlessly to the ground. Kendra gasped. How had her uncle managed to get to Jinx's side so quickly?

"Hurry," Uncle Griffinskitch ordered the grasshopper. "Get out of here!"

"I'm not going anywhere," Jinx shot back, pulling out another sword.

"The box!" Uncle Griffinskitch shouted. "Protect the box!"

Kendra had heard that tone from her uncle countless times. It meant, "No arguing!" Jinx seemed to know that too, for she turned and bounded down the passageway on her long, powerful legs. In the next moment, she had joined Kendra and the others at the end of the corridor, trapped against the door.

"There's no way through!" Professor Bumblebean told the grasshopper frantically. "The door is too heavy to open, and there's no room under it either."

Jinx gritted her teeth and with all her strength hurled herself at the door—but it didn't budge. With a fury, she threw herself at it again, but its massive timbers showed no response. "It's no use," she finally wheezed.

But Kendra barely heard her, for now she turned her eyes back to her uncle, down at the other end of the passage. The old white wizard had raised his crooked staff, and was holding it before Rumor.

"Now what's he doing?" Oki said.

"He's going to fight him," Kendra said.

"Out of my way, old man," the dragon snarled, smoke swirling out of his nostrils.

"Humph," Uncle Griffinskitch muttered in reply. It was the type of humph that meant he wasn't impressed.

"FINE," Rumor growled. With a snap of his tail, he struck the ceiling and sent a shower of stones crashing towards the old Een wizard.

"He'll be crushed!" Kendra screamed.

But Uncle Griffinskitch didn't even blink. His staff flashed and the falling stones suddenly changed to soft white snowflakes, settling gently upon the ground.

"You're starting to annoy me," Rumor hissed.

"Humph," Uncle Griffinskitch grunted, his eyes ablaze. The dragon came at him again, and this time his long pink tongue zipped out and curled around the wizard like a rope.

"He's going to swallow him whole!" Kendra screamed.

Without thinking, she started to run towards her uncle, but Jinx grabbed her by the leg and pinned her to the wall.

"Just keep out of his way," the grasshopper uttered. "He's up to something."

But it didn't seem like it to Kendra. Her uncle didn't seem to move a muscle, even though his hand and staff were free. Kendra held her breath as she watched the dragon pull the old Een right inside his gaping mouth. Then, at the last possible moment, Uncle Griffinskitch flicked his staff and fired a mighty zap of lightning down Rumor's long throat.

The dragon shrieked, reeling back as blue lightning crackled through his mouth. As he sat there, stunned and smoking, Uncle Griffinskitch turned and hobbled down the passage as fast as his legs would carry him.

"Quickly, we only have a few moments," the wizard panted.

Kendra had never seen her uncle so spent. He was trembling head to foot, and beads of sweat were rolling down his face, which now had gone as white as his beard. She quickly rushed to his side and helped support him.

"We can't get through the door," Jinx told the wizard.

"I'll blow it open," Uncle Griffinskitch said, furrowing his brow. He lifted his staff, but it was clear he had not one spark of magic strength left in his now frail body. He collapsed to the floor in a heap.

Then Kendra heard a rumbling. It was Rumor. He had recovered from his injuries and was now lumbering down the hall, his great body smashing against the walls and sending sheets of dust and rubble to the ground. In only a matter of seconds, he was upon them.

"No more tricks!" the dragon growled angrily. "I want my box!"

Rumor smashed his tail against the ground, and the floor shook so hard that Kendra and her companions were tossed into the air. Before they could hit the ground again, the scaled beast stretched out his massive claw and caught them in his palm.

"Days of Een!" Uncle Griffinskitch gasped, as the dragon closed his long, bony talons about them. "I landed on my staff!" The flustered wizard reached beneath him and pulled out his staff. It was broken and useless.

"I've had enough of this!" Jinx cried angrily. She began pulling knives and daggers from her weapons belt, thrusting them one by one into the dragon's palm. But it didn't matter how strong she was or how hard she stabbed. Every weapon broke against Rumor's thick skin.

"It's of no avail," Professor Bumblebean told the grasshopper. "You're wasting yourself, Captain."

Kendra felt herself being lifted upward with the others. The scaled fingers of their prison opened and they found themselves staring into Rumor's large glimmering eyes.

"Annoying little creatures," he rasped. "Give me back my treasure!"

Kendra spoke before she had time to think better of it. "It's not your box. It's ours. It belongs to us Eens!"

"No!" Rumor said, reaching down with his crooked nails to snatch the box and key away from Kendra and Oki. "The box is definitely *mine!*"

Kendra was sure the dragon would crush the box, for it was so small, and he was so enormous. But in handling the tiny treasure, the beast seemed to have the gentlest of touch.

Kendra and the rest of the company were another matter. Rumor didn't seem to care at all if he hurt them, and while cradling the box ever so carefully in one hand, he roughly closed his other about the company, plunging them back into total darkness.

Kendra felt the dragon turn and slither through the castle. She tried to peer out of the cracks between the dragon's claws, but he was holding them so tightly that she couldn't see out. Then Jinx tried. Her head was just small enough to squeeze out between the cracks in their scaly prison.

"We're back in the treasure vault," Jinx relayed to Kendra and the others, and they could hear the coins and other riches crunch and jingle under the dragon's tremendous weight. "He's returning the box and key back to the pedestal."

"I'm sorry," Kendra heard Rumor tell the box affectionately. "Now you are back in your rightful place."

"I wonder what happened to Pugglemud," Professor Bumblebean said. "Can you see him, Captain?"

"Yes, there he is!" Jinx whispered excitedly. "I can see him hiding behind a large mirror in the corner."

"I guess even he knows enough to hide," Kendra said.

"Shhh," Uncle Griffinskitch warned, still trembling with exhaustion. "The dragon might hear us."

But Rumor started moving again, and their voices were muffled by the sound of treasure crunching beneath him.

"Do you think Pugglemud can see you?" Kendra asked Jinx.

"I don't know," Jinx said. "I have to get his attention somehow. I hate to say it, but he might be the only one to save us now."

"Throw something down there so he knows we're here," Oki suggested.

Jinx pulled her head back in and looked about the enclosed fist. Most of their possessions had been lost during their capture, but Professor Bumblebean had managed to hang onto two of his precious books.

"Oh, don't you dare!" the professor cried when he saw what Jinx was thinking. "Elder Griffinskitch—don't let her!"

"We have no other way," the old wizard panted.

"Oh, my ancestors would be horrified," the professor sighed, handing over *The Illustrated History of Krodos*. Jinx took the hefty book, squeezed it out between Rumor's claws, and let it fall. With a clatter, it landed on the gold-covered floor.

Rumor did not hear the sound over his own footsteps, but Pugglemud noticed the book. He peered from behind the mirror and looked at the book curiously. Then, he gazed up at the dragon and spotted Jinx's head sticking out of Rumor's fist.

"He's seen us," Jinx reported.

"Good work, Captain," Uncle Griffinskitch said. "Let's hope he helps us."

Then, they felt Rumor turn and rumble out of the vault.

"Where's he taking us?" Oki asked.

At last the dragon came to a stop. He opened his fist, and Kendra noticed they were in a room with still more gold and riches, but also with dozens of cages of all different sizes, scattered haphazardly about the mounds of treasure. Rumor found a silver cage to his liking and tossed Kendra and the rest of the company inside. With a flick of his long tongue, he slammed the door shut.

"Welcome to the chamber of cages," he said, glaring upon them with his large yellow eyes. "This is what happens to those who try to steal my treasures!"

Kendra looked up at the beast. His eyes seemed to glimmer with self-satisfaction, and it angered her.

"You're not so tough," she declared, stepping to the front of the cage. "It's easy to pick on us. We're just tiny."

"Is that so?" the dragon responded, the smoke curling out of his nostrils.

"Kendra," Uncle Griffinskitch murmured softly from behind her. "It's okay. This isn't the time for your boldness. Don't anger him."

But Kendra couldn't help herself. She felt that tiny spark in her rise up. It was the same type of spark that had grabbed hold of her on the night when she had rescued Trooogul. She could not help but to act, and in this case, that meant giving the dragon a piece of her mind. "What about the giants?" she demanded of Rumor. "You're just their lackey, aren't you? Shouldn't you at least take us before your masters?"

"WHAT?" Rumor screamed (and the very bars on their cage rattled). "What masters do you think I have, teenie Eenie? Who do you think is more powerful than I?"

His tongue flicked out angrily, hitting Kendra and knocking her right to the floor of the cage.

"Kendra!" Uncle Griffinskitch cried helplessly.

Jinx helped Kendra to her feet, and the young girl turned and looked at Rumor once more. "I thought there were giants here," she said, feeling even braver, now that Jinx was at her side. "Where are they?"

"Giants? There are no giants here, my friends," Rumor hissed, with a particularly nasty emphasis on the word friends. "There haven't been for over seven hundred years."

"My word!" Professor Bumblebean exclaimed. He had been held speechless with fear since being tossed into the cage, but now his curiosity got the better of him. "What happened to the giants?" he asked. "I thought the castle of Krodos belonged to them."

"It belongs to ME," Rumor sneered. "I rid this castle of the giants and their gang of cronies long ago, back when the land of Een was but a child."

"So it was you alone who stole the Box of Whispers," Uncle Griffinskitch said.

"I didn't steal it," Rumor said, his long tongue flickering out warningly. "I tell you, I took what was mine."

"Humph," Uncle Griffinskitch grunted. "Then what do you mean to do with us?"

"Are you going to e-e-eat us?" Oki stammered anxiously.

Rumor lifted his great head and laughed so hard that they shook once again within their cage.

"Of course not!" the dragon said. "I would never eat such

disgusting little creatures as you! The very thought of you in my belly makes me ill. I have no use of your flesh. You see, I feed on something quite different."

"And what's that?" Kendra asked.

"I'll tell you," Rumor said with a wicked twinkle in his eye. "It's *fear*." And with that, the red dragon turned and slithered out of the chamber, back into his endless rooms of treasure.

"Did he say fear?" Jinx asked.

"He did," the professor replied. "I do say, I've never come across such nonsense in my studies. How does he exist on fear? The fear of what, I wonder?"

"Humph," Uncle Griffinskitch grunted. "The fear we have of him, I imagine."

"If that's the case, then he must feel like he just ate a ten-course dinner," Oki said, trembling from head to tail. "I've never been so afraid in my life!"

CHAPTER 21

Prisoners of Rumor

For two days and nights, Kendra and the rest of the company lay in the silver cage, amidst the piles of treasure, without so much as a visit from the dragon. Even so, they knew he was never far, for the castle often rumbled with his presence. They had no food, very little water (only Kendra and Jinx had managed to hang onto their canteens during their capture), and try as they might, they had no way of escaping. At first, Kendra harbored a hope that Pugglemud would come to their rescue, but they saw no sign of the scraggly Dwarf.

Kendra had never felt so miserable. Her stomach ached with hunger, and she spent hours on end gazing out at the dimly lit vault that stretched before their prison. There were countless cages scattered about the chamber, most of them filled with the skeletons of desperate thieves that Kendra imagined had come seeking the dragon's gold over the centuries. They had probably all perished from hunger and thirst, surrounded by the very treasure they had come to thieve. Now their remains hung limply out of their cages, tattered clothes and rotting skin hanging from their bones, and more than a few of their skeletal claws still reaching out in vain towards the glittering floor. Many of them seemed to be staring at Kendra with their giant vacant eye sockets, as if to taunt her.

"We'll end up just like them," Kendra murmured, rubbing her ravenous stomach.

"We must try to remain positive," Professor Bumblebean said, lifting his eyes from *The Comparative Book of Creatures from Beyond the Magic Curtain*, the only book he had left in his possession.

"I don't know how you can keep reading that thing day after day," Jinx grumbled irritably as she paced about the cage. "Kendra's right. We're just going to end up skeletons like everyone else in this wretched prison, Bumblebones."

"Hunger is obviously driving you insane," the professor replied. "For, after all we've been through, you're still getting my name wrong! It's Bumblebean, you know. I am a scholar, like my ancestors before me, and reading is what I do best. Besides, I'm sure, Captain Jinx, that if you were in possession of your sword, you would have polished it down to the size of a needle."

"If I had my sword, I would have hacked our way out of here by now," the grasshopper retorted.

"Humph," Uncle Griffinskitch grunted. "Such bickering will not save us." He himself had spent the better part of the last two days, recovering his strength and waving his hand over his broken staff, chanting strangely. According to the old wizard, it was a way to mend his staff, and he now closed his eyes to begin another round of incantations.

"Is it fixed yet?" Kendra asked when the old Een opened his eyes a few minutes later.

"Not yet," her uncle replied. "It takes a long time to mend magic things, if it can be done at all."

Kendra sighed. She was going crazy. Even sleep was of little comfort to her, for each time she drifted off, it was only to hear the dragon's voice, inside her dreams, chanting, "Een has helped Unger!" over and over again.

"Even if we get out, what will we do then?" Oki asked Uncle Griffinskitch. "If we try to take the Box of Whispers again, we still have to get past the dragon somehow."

"I say we leave the box behind," Jinx declared. "Let's just get away from this castle. Once we're back home, we can raise a proper army and attack the dragon in full force!"

"We cannot abandon the box," Uncle Griffinskitch said without hesitation.

"Why not?" Jinx demanded. "What's so important about it that it's worth risking our lives?"

"It is vital that we recover it," the old Wizard replied.

"But why?" Kendra asked. "It's just a box after all."

"It's not the box that's special," Uncle Griffinskitch said. "It's what's inside it."

"And that is?" Kendra persisted.

"It is a matter for elders only," the bearded old wizard said.

"Please," Kendra implored. "Look at everything we've been through, Uncle Griffinskitch. We could die in this cage, and we won't even know what for! Don't you think we deserve to know what's in the box?"

She paused and watched her uncle's bushy eyebrows furrow, as if he was in deep thought.

"For what it's worth, I agree with Kendra," Jinx said.

"I'm afraid I do as well," Professor Bumblebean spoke up.

"And me," Oki squeaked.

"Very well," Uncle Griffinskitch said finally, releasing a long sigh. "Listen, what I'm about to reveal to you is known only to the Council of Elders. So guard this well!"

"We will," Kendra assured her uncle.

"The Box of Whispers harbors a secret," Uncle Griffinskitch declared. "A very important secret—one that could mean the end of Een."

"I do say!" Professor Bumblebean exclaimed. "What is it?"

"It is the secret of the magic curtain," the old wizard replied gravely.

"What do you mean?" Kendra asked.

"The magic spell that makes the curtain work," Uncle Griffinskitch explained. "If the secret of this spell falls into the wrong hands, then the curtain could fall down."

"Fall down!" Oki cried.

"Yes," Uncle Griffinskitch said. "All of Een could be destroyed!"

"My word!" Professor Bumblebean gasped.

"That is why we must retrieve the box," Uncle Griffinskitch said. "We cannot risk the secret of the curtain being discovered."

Kendra sat down in the corner of the cage and sighed. "Well, this certainly changes things," she said. "We have to get that box—or else die trying!"

She had no sooner spoken when the chamber of cages began to tremble.

"Eek!" Oki cried, scurrying to the back of the cage. "It's Rumor!"

They watched and listened as the dragon approached. When he finally entered the chamber of cages, he seemed larger than they remembered, moving slowly through the room and knocking over mounds of treasure with his giant, reckless body. It was clear to see that he had captured someone else, for his fist was clenched in a tight ball. He slithered past the prisoners and emptied his claws into a nearby cage.

"Pugglemud!" Kendra exclaimed when she saw the hapless Dwarf roll out of the dragon's fist. Rumor smiled, and with a flicker of his tongue, shut the door to Pugglemud's cage. Kendra could barely believe her eyes—the Dwarf was dirtier and more ragged than ever. Gold coins were spilling out of every pocket (of which he had many), and his red hair was even more wild and tangled than before.

"I wondered what happened to you," Jinx called to Pugglemud. "You were supposed to help us out, you know."

At the sound of the grasshopper's voice, Rumor turned and hissed.

"You know this little beast?" the dragon snarled. "Horrible little creatures, these Dwarves. Just as greedy as Goojuns and Ungers. They're always coming after my treasure. You'd think they'd have learned by now, over these seven hundred years. But no, they keep trying. But has any thief escaped my watchful eye? No! Oh, yes, many are able to sneak inside the castle. And some I even let find the vault. But I don't let anyone out. It's all a game, but make no mistake: I'm the one controlling it!"

The dragon chuckled, and his breath felt like a roasting wind on Kendra's face.

"Oh, please lemme out!" Pugglemud begged, clenching the bars of his cage. "I learned me lesson, Mr. Dragon. I am done—I swear it. I'll never touch another piece o' gold so long as I live."

"LIAR!" Rumor roared.

There were no "tee-hees" from Pugglemud now. Large tears streamed down his dirty face, leaving long, clean trails on his cheeks.

"You know," Rumor said, turning back to the company's cage, "I had forgotten all about you pitiful creatures."

"Seems like you forget about all your prisoners," Jinx

declared boldly, pointing to some of the other cages where the skeletons lay.

"Oh, those," Rumor said. "Yes, well, as I said, Goojuns and Ungers and such. A little more dangerous than your kind." He lowered his head, and with a zip of his tongue, ripped the door from their cage so that it drooped lazily on one hinge. "You're free to go," he announced. "You are no threat to me. So run back to your little land, and tell the rest of your wretched friends to leave me and my property alone!"

Uncle Griffinskitch stepped to the edge of the cage and stared into the eyes of the immense dragon. "We are not going without the Box of Whispers," the wizard declared in a steely voice, though Kendra noticed that he was trembling.

"Then you will go nowhere," Rumor chuckled. "For the box is mine, and it will stay here."

"It belongs to the Eens," Uncle Griffinskitch said. "Let us have it. You have many treasures. Why do you care about one tiny box?"

"You're right about my wealth," Rumor gloated. "Look about you. I have gold as far as the eye can see. More treasure than you could count in a lifetime. Trinkets, baubles, and all manner of curios have I collected. But nothing is more important to me than the Box of Whispers. I would give away all of my other wealth for it."

"Still, the box is not yours to keep," Uncle Griffinskitch told the dragon. "It belongs to the Eens, and we mean to take it back."

"NO, THE BOX IS MINE, I TELL YOU!" Rumor roared, so loud that their cage rattled. He prowled menacingly before them, his nostrils flaring angrily with smoke. "Why don't you scurry back to your tiny land, back to the rest of your frightened,

foolish little folk?" Rumor growled. "You think you are so wise, with your Council of Elders. More like a council of buffoons! You think you know so much about the box, but I tell you—you can't begin to imagine its power!"

"I believe I have a pretty good idea," the tiny wizard said with determination.

"You're a fool," Rumor sneered. "A whiskered little fool."

"You don't frighten me," Uncle Griffinskitch declared. "No power shall you steal from me."

Rumor narrowed his yellow eyes at the wizard. "You really are quite clueless, aren't you?" the dragon asked with a chuckle. He was silent for the next few moments, as if in deep thought, and the only sound in the chamber was that of the beast's long pink tongue, flickering in and out.

"I tell you what, Gregor," Rumor said finally, and Kendra was surprised that the dragon knew his name. "I will make you a proposal. A wager, if you will. Each of you will come before me, one at a time, and take a test. If any of you can succeed, then you may take the box and go free."

"And if we don't?" Uncle Griffinskitch said.

"Well, I don't set the punishment if you fail. In a way, you do," Rumor said wickedly. Then he added, as though he were offering them a great gift, "But listen, you don't all have to succeed. Just one of you; then you all go free."

"That is all?" Uncle Griffinskitch asked. "We solve your

test, and then we can go free? And with the box?"

"That is the deal," Rumor said. "But I know you Eens and your little animal friends all too well. You are weak. You will all fail."

"We shall see," Uncle Griffinskitch said defiantly.

"Indeed, we shall," Rumor said. "Well, I must be on my way. When you hear the crash of my gong, the first of you may come before me in the vault of riches. I believe you know the way, being thieves and all. And remember, only one at a time."

The dragon turned and rumbled away, his shoulders scraping the sides of the chamber as he went.

"Lemme out, lemme out!" Pugglemud begged, as soon as the dragon was gone. "Don't leave me in this cage!"

"Why would we help you?" Jinx growled. "You certainly had no intention of helping us! We've been sitting here for two days."

"I was goin' to help you," Pugglemud said. "I was on my way when I got captured."

"Nonsense!" Jinx scowled. "The only thing you care about is gold."

"How could we let you out?" Kendra asked the Dwarf. "We don't have a key for your cage, and we're sure not strong enough to bust it open."

"Oh, I'm in a sorry way," Pugglemud wailed.

"I do say, Elder Griffinskitch," Professor Bumblebean said, turning his attention away from the Dwarf. "I don't know about this contest. Do you think this game with Rumor is such a good idea?"

"Humph," the old wizard grunted in reply. Professor Bumblebean shrugged, but Kendra knew what her uncle meant with that humph. He was saying: "Do you have a better plan?"

CHAPTER 22

The Trial
of Whispers

The gong of the dragon sounded only a few moments later.

"It's time already!" Kendra cried.

"My word," Professor Bumblebean remarked. "He's certainly not giving us much time to prepare, is he?"

"I don't need to prepare," Jinx declared. "I'll be back before you know it."

"What are you talking about, Captain?" the professor exclaimed. "You're not going first."

"Of course I am," Jinx said.

"May I remind you," Professor Bumblebean said, "that I am our best authority on magical creatures. As such, I believe I will proceed first."

"Oh, you pompous, overblown word nerd," Jinx snapped. "What are you going to do, Blatherbean? Bonk him with your book?"

"This is no time to argue," Uncle Griffinskitch said. "I am an elder, the only one here. Therefore, I will go first."

"You are both forgetting one important thing," Jinx said.

"And what's that?" Professor Bumblebean demanded.

"As captain of the Een guard and official protector of the elders, it's my duty to face any danger first," Jinx replied.

"That may be," Professor Bumblebean said, "but this is a special situation."

"Nonetheless, I intend to fulfill my duty," Jinx defended.

Just then the gong rang a second time.

"Humph," Uncle Griffinskitch muttered. "Regrettably, Captain Jinx is right. It is her duty to go first."

"I must tell you, Elder Griffinskitch, I disagree with this course of action," Professor Bumblebean said.

"So noted," Uncle Griffinskitch said, turning to Jinx. "Captain, I don't trust the dragon, but I do trust your bravery. Draw on your courage, and you may defeat that red devil."

"It'll all be over soon," Jinx said.

Then, with her head held high, Jinx hopped out of the cage and quickly left the chamber. Kendra and the others waited in anxious silence, but only a few minutes passed before the gong sounded again.

"My word!" Professor Bumblebean cried. "Jinx has failed, and all too quickly!"

"What happened to her?" Kendra cried.

But no one could answer.

"I'm going next," Uncle Griffinskitch declared.

"Oh, please be careful," Kendra said, clutching the old Een's sleeve.

"Try not to worry," Uncle Griffinskitch said, squeezing her by the shoulder. "You'll be okay."

"What do you mean?" Kendra cried, feeling a surge of panic. "Don't talk like that! You sound like you're not coming back."

Uncle Griffinskitch drew close. "Listen," he whispered in her ear. "I've got to go now. But somehow I can't help feeling that you will have a part to play in all of this yet. You're headstrong and curious, Kendra. I think that's why the orb chose you for this trip. So remember these qualities. They may save you yet."

And with these parting words, he shuffled out of the cage and towards the vault of riches.

"What happens if we all fail?" Oki asked after the old wizard had parted.

"I don't know," Professor Bumblebean admitted. "I'm sure Elder Griffinskitch will succeed. And if for some reason his magic does not prevail, my intellect surely will."

Kendra wasn't sure if these words offered any comfort to Oki, but there was nothing they could do other than wait. The three companions climbed out of the cage and paced nervously back and forth in the sea of gold coins that carpeted the floor. After their long imprisonment, it felt good to stretch their legs. All the while, Pugglemud wailed and complained, but Kendra did her best to ignore him.

Then, suddenly, the gong rang again.

Professor Bumblebean let out a deep sigh and shook his head sadly.

"Uncle Griffinskitch!" Kendra exclaimed. "Why don't they come back, Professor? What's happening?"

"I don't know," Professor Bumblebean said with a gulp. "Well, it's my turn now, I suppose."

"The dragon's winning!" Kendra said. "We have to do something."

"Well, if there was ever anything that a Bumblebean was meant to do, it was to pass a test," the professor said, pushing up his glasses with determination. "I'm sure I will triumph in this malicious game, so don't fret. I will soon return with your uncle and the captain both."

He bent down and gave Kendra and Oki an uncharacteristic hug. Then he was gone, and now it was just the three of them—Kendra, Oki, and Pugglemud, who was still loudly blubbering and bemoaning his fate.

The waiting was the worst thing. Kendra couldn't help thinking of her uncle. He had obviously failed the trial. But with what consequence?

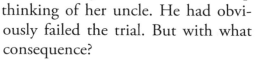

"Do you think Bumblebean will do it?" Oki asked Kendra.

"I just don't know," she said. "I wish I knew what to expect in there. Maybe then we'd have some clue as to how to defeat the dragon."

"Kendra, if Bumblebean fails, I want to go next," Oki said. "I don't want to sit here all alone with Pugglemud."

"No, I think I should go," Kendra said. "My uncle is an elder after all."

"So what?" Oki said. "I work after school for the elders. So I should go."

The two friends argued over the subject until they were interrupted by the bang of the gong.

"Oh, no!" Oki cried. "Now what will we do?"

"C'mon," Kendra said. "Let's flip one of these gold coins. Whoever wins the toss can go."

"Okay," Oki agreed. "I choose heads."

Kendra picked up one of the large gold coins and heaved it into the air. She and Oki followed it with earnest gazes as it flipped through the air and landed with a clink at their feet.

"Tails," Kendra announced. "I go first."

"Drat," Oki said.

Just then they heard the gong again.

"I better go, Oki," Kendra said. "But listen, I have an idea. Why don't you wait a few minutes, then follow me? Maybe you can learn what happens inside the vault and use it against Rumor."

"Wouldn't that be cheating?" Oki asked.

"I don't know," Kendra said. "But we have to try something, don't we? We're just kids. I don't know if we can pass this trial unless we help each other."

"Okay," Oki said. "Let's do it."

"Bye for now," Kendra said, hugging her friend tightly.

"Good luck," Oki murmured.

"Thanks," Kendra said and, with a nervous gulp, she turned and left the chamber.

CHAPTER 23

Kendra Goes Next

Sometimes

it's best not to know what awaits you around life's next corner. This was certainly true in Kendra's case, for if she had known what she was about to face, she may have just run away. But all she could think of now was somehow saving her friends and her uncle, and it was this hope that forced her tiny feet down the long passageway that led to the vault of riches.

She could hear Rumor's voice inside her head as she drew closer: "Een has helped Unger! Een has helped Unger!" Kendra tried to tune the voice out. She needed her mind to be clear. When she reached the glittering vault, she paused and peeked inside.

There was the dragon, nestled comfortably in his pile of gold and treasures, with his tail curled tightly about his body. To Kendra's astonishment, he was considerably larger than the last time she had seen him, only a short time ago. In front of Rumor, resting on its pedestal, sat the Box of Whispers. It pulsed with a warm, radiant glow that bathed the entire vault in light.

"Well, don't linger there all day, Kandlestar," Rumor said. Kendra was surprised that he could see her and even more surprised that he knew her name. She was so tiny, after all, and the vault was so enormous. Timidly, she approached the dragon. She had only gone a few steps, however, when she saw Captain Jinx standing in front of her, facing the Box of Whispers.

"Captain Jinx!" Kendra called, running up to her.

But when the grasshopper didn't reply, Kendra realized that it wasn't Jinx at all, but rather a statue that looked like her. In fact, it looked exactly like her.

"W-what's going on?" Kendra asked.

Rumor roared with laughter.

Then Kendra looked ahead and saw the figure of Professor Bumblebean standing closer to the box and, even closer, a statue of Uncle Griffinskitch. Both statues were made completely from stone, just like Jinx's statue. Kendra stared at the figure of Uncle Griffinskitch. Every wisp of his beard, every detail, had been sculpted to perfection. Then the horrible truth slowly sunk in. This wasn't just a statue of her uncle. It *was* her uncle. He, along with Captain Jinx and Professor Bumblebean, had somehow been turned to stone. Kendra might as well have been struck by lightning—the shock was the same. She fell to the ground, speechless and horrified. There her uncle and

companions stood, frozen in mid-movement, expressions of surprise forever captured on each of their faces. Their eyes, now cold and stony, stared blankly ahead.

"W-what's happened?" Kendra sobbed. "What did you do to them?"

Rumor stifled his laughter and glared down at the small Een. "Why, I have done nothing, Kendra," the dragon replied in mock innocence.

"But they've been turned to stone!" Kendra cried, feeling the tears roll down her cheeks.

"Yes, indeed, but not by me," Rumor said. "They have been petrified, Kendra, petrified by their own fears. You see, they were in control of their own fate, just as you are."

"You tricked them," Kendra accused.

"No, Kendra, not I," the dragon replied, slithering closer to her. His long tongue flickered out, tickling her cheek.

"You see," Rumor said, "my test is simple: go into the Box of Whispers and face what is there."

"That doesn't make sense," Kendra sniffled. "The only thing in there is the . . ."

"The secret of the magic curtain?" Rumor interrupted. "Yes, that's one of the things."

"One of the things!" Kendra cried. "What do you mean?"

"And now you shall know the truth about the Box of Whispers," Rumor glowered. "It just doesn't hold that one secret. It holds *all* the secrets of Een!"

The Dragon laughed at Kendra's look of shock. "That's right, young Kandlestar," he hissed. "Every single secret ever kept since the dawn of your pathetic little land is recorded inside the box. As soon as someone forges a secret, the box knows about it. Some of the secrets are deep and dark. Some are frivolous. Some are secrets no one would ever care about; others would mean the very ruin of Een. But to the box, all the secrets are the same. It protects each and every one. Even yours, Kendra."

"M-m-mine?" Kendra stammered.

"Yes," Rumor replied, his pleasure all too apparent. "See, all I ask is that you go into the box and take out your secret, the truth that is hidden there, deep inside its magical belly. Can you do that, Kendra? Can you confront your secret? For your friends could not. The trial of whispers was too great for them!"

"Who are you to hold our secrets?" Kendra asked bravely. "Why should we not keep our secrets if we so please?"

Rumor laughed and circled about Kendra. "Then keep them, Kandlestar," he hissed. "Make the same mistake that all the Eens have made since the dawn of time!"

Kendra trembled as she stared up into the dragon's gleaming yellow eyes. "What do you mean?" she asked. "What do you know of the ancient Eens?"

"Would you like to hear *my* secret, Kendra?" Rumor asked. "Never mind, I will tell you anyway. You see, I know everything about the Eens, because, my little friend, I am an Een!"

Kendra could not believe her ears. "No!" she cried. "That's not true! That's impossible!"

Rumor towered over the fallen girl. "No, Kandlestar," the dragon growled. "I think you know it's the truth. How else could I get through the magic curtain? Only Eens can do that. I tell you, I am an Een, because after all, it was the Eens who made me."

"No! No!" Kendra sobbed. "We would never make a monster like you!"

"Oh, it was not on purpose, I assure you," Rumor explained. "You see, over a thousand years ago, the ancient Eens made the magic curtain to protect their land from the outside world. And they put the secret of the curtain into the Box of Whispers, to keep it safe. But they enchanted the box too strongly. You understand, Kandlestar, that the box was meant to hold only the secret of the curtain. But its magic was so powerful that it absorbed every secret kept by every Een, no matter how small, no matter how insignificant."

"I know all about secrets," Kendra retorted, thinking of Trooogul.

"Of course you do," Rumor said. "But do you know how powerful secrets are, Kendra? To what lengths we will go, just to protect them? And what do you think happened to the Box of Whispers as it tried to absorb more and more secrets? The power became too great. The box could not contain the darkness of so many whispers. And deep within the Elder Stone, where the Eens kept the Box of Whispers, there was another magical object. Do you know what that was?"

"No," Kendra said miserably.

"An egg," the dragon replied, with a long, wicked grin. "A simple egg, laid by a dragon. An egg that the elders had long ago forgotten about. But the egg began to grow with life, Kendra. It grew with the power fed to it by the Box of Whispers, which lay no more than a coin's toss away. And once the ancient Eens realized this, they took the egg and cast it into the wilds of the outside world, hoping to never see its darkness hatch. But they were too late. For it did hatch, Kandlestar . . . it did hatch."

"And you were born," Kendra guessed.

"Exactly," Rumor said. "So, you see, the box is mine. It fed me with the power of all the secrets of Een, as numberless as the grains of sand that line the ocean. The ancient Eens even named me, you know. I could hear them, as I grew inside the egg. They couldn't bring themselves to say the word 'dragon,' so they said things like: 'Have you heard the rumor? The rumor about the egg?' and 'What will we do about this rumor?' So, you see, I naturally thought Rumor was my name."

"Why didn't you come back to Een sooner?" Kendra asked.

"Well, I couldn't find it, for one thing," Rumor replied, seeming rather pleased that she had asked. "After all, I was in an egg when I was taken away, so I couldn't exactly mark the spot. For a thousand years, I combed the lands, searching for the box. And during that time, I amused myself by collecting all the treasures known to man and monster. Gold. Diamonds. Precious stones. Everything that gives the greedy the urge to steal and the wicked the desire to murder. But always my box was calling to me. It is like my parent, after all. So why should I not have it?"

"But how did you get the box?" Kendra asked, her voice desperate and sad.

"I discovered the magic curtain at long last," Rumor replied. "And lo and behold, I could go through it, like any other Een. At last, I was able to take what was rightfully mine! At last, after a thousand years, the Box of Whispers and I have been reunited!"

Kendra's head drooped to the floor. It was too much for her to bear.

"And now you know one of the darkest secrets kept by the elders for all these years," Rumor said. "The ancient Eens knew I was connected to the box, and still they cast my egg into the wilderness, hoping that I would never come back to haunt them. It's a secret the elders have been passing down for years, generation after generation. The elders have tried to ignore the truth. They never talk about me. But they know, Kendra, they know. Even your dear old Uncle Griffinskitch."

"But how can you tell this secret?" Kendra demanded. "It's not yours to reveal!"

"Why not?" Rumor chortled. "The box and I are one! I know every secret in the box, and I can be its voice, if I so choose. But don't worry, I've told you but one secret. I can tell you others that are far more tantalizing. How about your uncle's? That one has to do with your mother."

"My mother!" Kendra exclaimed.

"Indeed," Rumor said. "You see, ten years ago, your mother had a fight with her brother, your very own Uncle Griffinskitch. Your mother was a sorceress, just as Griffinskitch is a wizard. Your mother was quite a bit younger than your uncle, but like so many brothers and sisters, they were always trying to best the other. Ah yes, your mother was a fiery sort, I imagine. She was always challenging your uncle. And one day, they had a terrible fight. I suppose old Griffinskitch said unkind words, much too unkind to even repeat. And so your mother left Een to go fight the monsters of the outside world and to prove herself to your uncle. Naturally, your father and brother went to find her. But none of them ever returned."

"What happened to them?" Kendra asked, her throat catching with a hope she didn't know she had been harboring. It was the hope that maybe, just maybe, Rumor would know where her family was.

But he did not. "I have no idea," Rumor told Kendra, with a cruel shrug. "Nor do I really care. They disappeared and you were left in the care of old Griffinskitch. And now you know the secret that has consumed him for ten years. It is a secret that carries the burden of something else—guilt. I imagine he feels it every time he casts his old eyes upon you, for you only serve to remind him of how he drove away his own sister."

Kendra stared at the floor, crying. Was it possible, she wondered, that this was the reason her uncle was always so gruff with her? Because he was guilty? Kendra felt as if her whole life was turning upside down.

"And how about your companions' secrets?" Rumor continued. "Shall I reveal them, too?"

"No," Kendra said softly.

"I'll tell you, anyway," Rumor said with a long smirk, and he curled his long tail around Kendra in an almost affectionate manner. "First, there's your brave Captain Jinx. Well, simply put, she can't read. Not a word. And she was so embarrassed by it, she never told a soul. Not even her Uncle Jasper. And that's why she drank that magic potion, you know, because she just couldn't read the label!"

Kendra rubbed the tears from her eyes and remembered how angry Jinx had been that day on the road when Professor Bumblebean had questioned her about the potions. It was no wonder she bullied the professor so much. He had something she did not: the ability to read.

"Then, of course, there's Bumblebean himself," Rumor said. "Pompous fool, always bragging about his great lineage. Well, here's a secret for you: Bumblebean was adopted! That's right. So his story about coming from a long line of scholars is just that—a story!"

"My uncle! My friends!" Kendra sobbed, gazing over at the cold stone statues that had once been her companions.

"But you have your own secret," Rumor hissed with an accusing tone. "Your own deep, dark truth that you now must confront, Kandlestar."

Kendra stared up at the dragon. Rumor smiled back at her, a long wicked smile that curled up at the ends of his mouth.

"Into the box you go," Rumor commanded.

CHAPTER 24

The Power of Secrets

Rumor lowered his snout and breathed a strange, perfumed cloud into Kendra's face. She felt her mind grow foggy and heavy, like she was entering a dream. Her eyes flickered and closed. When she opened them, only a moment later, she found herself in a strange, dimly lit room. There was dust everywhere, as thick as a blanket of snow. Except Kendra normally thought of snow as making everything seem fresh and new, but this room didn't smell fresh at all. It smelled old, older than all of time.

As Kendra stood there, her eyes adjusting to the darkness, she became aware of a strange and faint murmuring. It was the room, Kendra realized. The very walls seemed alive with a thousand whispers.

"What is this place?" Kendra exclaimed out loud. "Where am I?"

Then Rumor's voice came to her. "You're inside the Box of Whispers, Kendra. At least your mind is. Your body is still here with me, in the vault of riches."

"I'm in two places at once?" Kendra asked.

"I hardly expected you to understand," Rumor snapped. "You're dreaming, in a way. And inside your dream you're in the Box of Whispers."

Kendra didn't feel like she was dreaming. The box seemed real enough. But she knew some sort of strange magic was occurring, for there was no other way that she could fit inside the Box of Whispers.

Then she heard Rumor again. "Go to your secret, Kendra!"

Kendra looked about the box but couldn't see anything besides some dusty shelves that lined the walls. She cautiously approached the nearest shelf and, upon clearing away some of the dust and cobwebs, found herself staring at a row of tiny bottles. Then she noticed more shelves and more bottles, thousands of them, seemingly stretching on forever. Each bottle had a name on it. Scanning the bottles, she recognized some of the names: Honest Oki, Burdock Brown, Treewort Timm, to name a few. Then she saw her own bottle, clearly marked Kendra Kandlestar.

Rumor's voice once again filled the box. "Everyone has a secret, Kendra. Some have many. But you, Kendra, have only one. And yet it torments you, night and day. It invades your thoughts, curses your very dreams!"

Kendra reached up to the shelf with her little hand and lifted her bottle from its musty perch. She squinted through the faint light to gaze upon its contents. And there she saw a poisonous red cloud, swirling and glowing and sending an empty, hollow feeling into the pit of her stomach.

"And will you open it, Kendra?" Rumor asked. "Will you?"

Kendra gulped and put her hand on the cork that plugged the bottle. She began to twist the cork.

"Are you sure, Kendra?" she heard Rumor say, and she quickly lifted her hand from the stopper. "If you open the bottle, all of Een shall know your secret."

With a start, Kendra dropped the bottle. It landed on the floor, its fall broken by the carpet of dust. With a soft rattle, it rolled into the dark recesses of the box.

"Yes, Kendra," Rumor whispered. His voice felt so close, as if he were whispering right in her ear. "Open the bottle, and everyone will know that you helped an Unger!"

Kendra couldn't see the dragon, but she could imagine the dreadful beast with a long smirk spreading across his face. "Een has helped Unger!" he chanted. "Een has helped Unger! Een has helped Unger!"

The dragon's accusation grew louder and stronger, building inside the box until it became a mighty roar.

"STOP!" Kendra sobbed. "I didn't . . . I just tried to . . . I just wanted to help, that's all!"

"And is that what you'll tell the Council of Elders?" Rumor demanded angrily. "That you wanted to help an Unger? That you wanted to help one of the greatest enemies known to Een? Indeed, what will they do with you, Kendra, the curious little girl who is always asking questions, stirring up trouble? What will your uncle and the elders do when they learn you committed the gravest crime for an Een? I'll tell you what they'll do! They will cast you from Een, and you will be left to wander the outside world, shunned and alone!"

"No!" Kendra cried. "Don't tell them! Don't tell them!"

And as she said these last words, Kendra felt herself leaving the box and returning to her body. But her body was no longer the same. She felt cold, and her hands and pointed ears began to go numb. She wanted to wiggle her nose, but it stiffened even as she tried. Her eyes felt like they were filling with hard grains of sand, and her vision began to fade. Then, to her horror, Kendra realized what was happening. She was turning to stone.

Now, through grainy eyes, Kendra could see Rumor laughing with wicked delight behind the Box of Whispers that still sat glowing on its pedestal. Even as he was laughing, the red dragon appeared to be growing. Kendra could feel him feeding from her fear, even as her own energy drained away, even as she turned slowly to stone. But how could he be growing? Kendra wondered. Rumor thrived on fear, but she didn't feel afraid of him. Not now. The only thing she was afraid of was her secret.

Then, it clicked, like a giant puzzle receiving its last and biggest piece; finally, Kendra realized the truth about Rumor. His power came from the fear of secrets, and with every secret that petrified an Een with fear, the dragon grew bigger and stronger. And, of course, every day someone in the land of Een hatched a secret, serious or otherwise. It was no surprise he grew bigger with each passing day.

Kendra's mind began to feel heavier and thicker. It was like having a cast on your arm or leg, but to Kendra it was as if the cast covered her entire body, from the tips of her long braids to her tiny feet. She wondered if Oki had felt something like this when he had been turned into an onion. She would never know, of course, for when would she ever talk to Oki again? She would be trapped forever within her prison of stone!

Then, as if he had somehow known she was thinking about him, Oki appeared before Kendra. She could barely see his small gray body, whiskery and timid, scurrying over the carpet of gold coins towards her.

"Kendra!" Oki squeaked.

Kendra tried to yell back, but her throat was too stiff and gravelly. But now she knew what to do. She knew what she had to say. She could feel her spark begin to shine, deep inside of her, and once it began to shine, there was no stopping her.

"Oki," she rasped, but her voice came out soft and muffled because her throat was turning to stone. "Oki," she repeated, and now the spark was building, and her voice was louder.

"What are you trying to do, Kandlestar?" Rumor demanded. Kendra could hear a panic in his voice, and it only gave her more strength. The spark was going to burst forth from her. She could feel it. She mustered the last of her strength, and the words came out even louder and clearer. "Oki!"

"Kendra! Kendra!" Oki called, still running towards her.

"I helped an Unger, Oki!" Kendra shouted. "I saved his life!"

Oki skidded to a halt, a few paces in front of Kendra, his eyes as wide as saucers.

"No! How can this be?" Rumor screeched, shaking his fist.

Even as the giant dragon roared, Kendra could feel the cold stone slipping away from her body. At last she could wriggle her fingers. At last she could twitch her pointed ears! She had told her secret and was free!

"Oki!" Kendra cried, rushing forward and embracing her friend.

"It's impossible!" Rumor screamed, rising to his full height and hovering over the two tiny friends. "You told your secret!"

"Yes," Kendra said. "Now release my uncle and friends and give me the Box of Whispers!"

"NEVER!" Rumor yelled.

"But we had a deal!" Kendra exclaimed.

"THE BOX IS MINE!" Rumor roared. "You can never have the box. And you won't have to worry about being expelled from Een, Kendra. I can promise you that. Because after I finish with you, I'm going to go tell every Unger, skarm, and other wretched beast I can find in this infernal world about the secret formula for the magic curtain. As soon as they get their claws on that whisper, I can assure you that Een will be nothing more than a wasteland!"

"How dare you!" Kendra demanded angrily.

"Don't worry, Kandlestar," Rumor hissed, rearing above her. "You won't be around to witness the destruction of your beloved land!"

"Watch out, Kendra!" Oki yelled.

With all his might, the small gray mouse pulled his friend behind a giant silver vase, just as Rumor unleashed a blazing jet of fire upon the gold-covered floor. The flames licked around them, scorching Kendra's braids and Oki's tail, but the vase protected them from the brunt of the dragon's attack. Quickly, they darted through the maze of treasure, trying to hide from Rumor.

"We have to get the box," Kendra gasped. She tried tugging her braids, but they were scorched and black, and they crumbled between her fingers.

"I think we have bigger problems right now," Oki said, coughing from the smoke of Rumor's outburst.

"No, don't you see?" Kendra said. "There are thousands of secrets in the box, and he feeds on them, on the fear we have of them. If we open the box, we'll take away his power."

"What in the name of onions are you talking about?" Oki asked.

"It's the only way, Oki. I'm sure of it!" Kendra insisted in a frantic whisper.

"Okay, okay," Oki conceded. "But how will we get to the box? As soon as we step into the open, that dragon will fry us."

"We'll split up," Kendra said. "You go one way, and I'll go another. He won't be able to get us both at the same time."

Kendra knew her little friend was so afraid that he couldn't even speak. But Oki took a deep breath and seemed to make up his mind. He nodded his approval of Kendra's plan, then squeezed her hand.

"Good luck," Kendra murmured.

"CURSE YOU!" Rumor howled as Kendra and Oki darted out from the mounds of treasure, each going a different direction.

The ferocious dragon curled his tail and brought it down against the ground with such force that a great crack opened up, right down the middle of the room. The floor creaked and groaned as each side of the chamber began to give way, sagging towards the center. Everything inside the vault—the gold, the jewels, even Kendra and Oki—began sliding towards the gaping hole.

"The box!" Kendra cried. "Where is it?"

Then she saw it, across the floor. It had been thrown from its pedestal by the force of Rumor's attack, and it was sliding towards the great opening. Without a second thought, Kendra dove over the avalanche of gold coins and wrapped her hands around the box, just as it was about to plunge into the depths below. It throbbed within her hands, but she held it tightly.

Kendra barely had a chance to let out a sigh of relief when Rumor sent his tail crashing to the floor again. The ground crumbled beneath Kendra. Still clutching the box in one arm, she pulled herself back as jewels, glimmering treasures, and thousands of gold coins disappeared over the lip of the crack into nothingness below. The sound was deafening.

Rumor breathed out more fire, and soon, there was so much smoke and dust in the chamber that Kendra could barely see. She closed her eyes against the stinging fumes, and when she next looked up, she saw the dragon hovering over her, his tail poised to flatten her.

"Careful!" Kendra cried, holding the box above her like a shield. "Would you really chance destroying the box?"

"And what good is it to you?" Rumor hissed. "You don't have the key."

For a moment, Kendra felt her heart drop, but she said boldly, "Neither do you!"

"I have it, Kendra," Oki shouted, and she looked up to see her tiny friend on the other side of the chasm. He began running towards her, the magic key clenched tightly in his paws.

"Look out for the hole, Oki!" Kendra cried. She could see that he meant to jump across it, but he was so tiny, and the crack so wide. She wanted to yell at him, to tell him that she didn't want him to risk it. There were so many things she wanted to tell him, her best friend in the whole world. But when she opened her mouth, only one thing came out. "DON'T THINK ABOUT ONIONS!" she yelled at the top of her lungs.

Oki leapt across the crack. How he was able to do it while clutching the key, Kendra never knew, but in the next instant, the tiny mouse landed next to her with a triumphant thud.

"Silly little fools!" Rumor growled, rearing back to scorch them with flames.

"It's now or never!" Kendra shouted to Oki.

Together, they grabbed the long key, and plunged it into the Box of Whispers.

CHAPTER 25

The Whispers Released

Kendra and Oki turned the key, and with a mighty "click," the lid of the box flew open, with a blinding flash of brilliant white light.

"NOOOOOOO!" Rumor howled.

The whispers burst forth from the box in a deafening roar, exploding with such force that Kendra and Oki were hurled across the room. They watched in awe as the secrets crackled and snapped like lightning, raging across the vault and ripping through the very walls. Even over the noise of everything else, they could hear the secrets tearing down the passages and halls of the castle, for indeed, they were no longer whispers, but mighty shrieks and wails. And Kendra and Oki could hear them clearly—all the secrets since the dawn of Een, revealing themselves as they escaped into the outside world. They were so loud that the sky boomed with their thunder, and Kendra knew they could be heard all the way home. "Luka Long-Ears forged a note from her mother!" "Skarab Strom cheated on his algebra exam!" "Honest Oki lied to the elders!"

There were thousands of secrets, so many that Kendra could not begin to hear or remember them all. The older secrets were not as clear as the newer ones, and were so faint that by the time the last of them escaped from the box, they were but whispers again.

But Kendra's secret was not there, for she had already set it free.

Rumor howled in agony as the secrets rippled over his giant body, tearing him to pieces, even as they fought their frantic course to freedom. Thrashing madly against the walls and pillars of the vault, the screeching, pain-stricken dragon began knocking massive wooden timbers and blocks of stone to the floor. The whole castle felt like it was crumbling. Then, in a sudden explosion of smoke, the giant dragon was gone.

Kendra and Oki exchanged a surprised glance, but there was hardly a moment to think about what had happened, for the room was still collapsing around them.

"We'll be crushed!" Oki shouted, narrowly avoiding a giant falling brick.

Then, Kendra thought she heard Uncle Griffinskitch's voice shouting to them from the smoky haze.

"Kendra!" the voice cried.

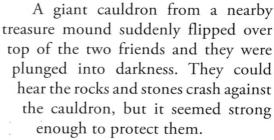

A giant cauldron from a nearby treasure mound suddenly flipped over top of the two friends and they were plunged into darkness. They could hear the rocks and stones crash against the cauldron, but it seemed strong enough to protect them.

"Did you hear Uncle Griffinskitch?" Kendra exclaimed.

"He's turned to stone," Oki said. "You must have imagined it."

"I guess you're right," Kendra said, and the thought splintered her heart with loss. She would never see her uncle, never learn anything more of her family. All seemed lost. Stricken with grief and exhaustion, she closed her eyes and listened to the rocks hammer against their makeshift shelter.

It seemed like hours later (though in truth, it was probably only a few minutes) when the rocks ceased smashing against the cauldron, and the thunderous noise of the collapsing room came to a halt.

"At least we didn't slide into that hole," Oki said. "All the treasure must have finally filled it up."

"C'mon," Kendra said, "let's get out from under here."

The two friends pushed and strained against the heavy cauldron, but try as they might, they could not lift it.

"Try grabbing it from underneath its lip," Oki said. They wedged their paws and fingers underneath the edge of the cauldron, but it simply wouldn't budge.

"We must be buried under a pile of rock and rubble," Oki said.

Kendra exhaled with exhaustion. She felt defeated. "Now what are we going to do?" she asked.

"We'll just have to wait for someone to rescue us," Oki replied.

"No one even knows we're here," Kendra said. Her uncle, Captain Jinx, and Professor Bumblebean had all been turned to stone. She and Oki would run out of air long before any rescue mission could be launched from Een. They would need a miracle.

The two young friends collapsed to the ground. They had been through so much together. Would their adventures end like this?

After a time, Kendra said, "Are you mad at me for helping the Unger?"

"No," the tiny mouse replied. "Why would I be?"

"Because I helped him!" Kendra exclaimed. "An Unger. Our enemy."

"I imagine it's a hard thing to let someone die," Oki said. After a moment's thought, he added, "Even an Unger. How could you not help him?"

But Kendra didn't seem any less glum.

"I have a secret," Oki said.

"I know," Kendra said. "I heard it fly from the box. You lied to the elders."

"Do you want to know what the lie was?" Oki asked.

"No," Kendra said.

"Well, we don't have anything better to do," the mouse said. "And it will take my mind off my scorched tail!"

"Okay," Kendra said, laughing in spite of herself.

"Well, my father had just gotten me the after-school job with the elders," Oki began. "And I did fine for the longest time. Then one day, I was supposed to deliver a message to Elder Brown from Treewort Timm. You know Treewort. He runs the shop down on Hoodoo Street with all the strange magic artifacts. He's about a hundred years old and most forgetful. Well, that particular day I lost the message."

"How?" Kendra asked.

"I don't know," Oki said with a shrug. "I just lost it. And I was so embarrassed because everyone was saying what a great job I was doing, and my father was so proud of me. So I just gave Elder Burdock a blank piece of parchment and when he unrolled it, I acted just as surprised as him. I told him that old Treewort must have forgotten to write his message down."

"But Treewort forgets things all the time," Kendra said, for she did indeed know the old Een and his habits.

"But not this time," Oki said. "So I just lied about it, and everyone had a good chuckle and blamed old Treewort. But it made me feel really bad. Especially since I'm supposed to be 'Honest Oki'."

"Oh, Oki," Kendra said. "It's hardly a secret. How does it compare to what I did?"

"Well, that secret has meant a lot to me over the past few months," Oki said. "It's kept me up at night, and in that way, it's just as bad as yours."

Kendra sighed. She could see Oki's point of view, but it still didn't make her feel any better. She closed her eyes and sighed again. She didn't want to talk about it any more. She wished she could just make it all go away. She pictured Uncle Griffinskitch, now turned to stone, and began to drift in and out of sleep, her head growing dizzy as the air supply diminished.

The next thing Kendra remembered was a ringing. At first, she thought it was just in her head, but then Oki said weakly, "Do you hear that, Kendra? It sounds like a bell."

They put their ears to the side of the cauldron, listening intently, and sure enough, they not only heard the ringing again, but the sound of someone rummaging around in the rubble above.

"Help!" Kendra yelled. "Get us out of here!"

"I'm coming!" came a reply.

"That voice sounds familiar," Oki said.

In the next moment, they heard a mighty grunt, and the cauldron tilted upwards under the strength of Ratchet's paws. Kendra and Oki breathed in the fresh new air as the rascally raccoon tossed the cauldron aside. Grinning ear to ear, he rushed forward and embraced his friends. He was still wearing the bewitched bell around his collar, and it was ringing excitedly.

"Now that we're all here, we can get this party going," Ratchet declared.

"Not much of a party with only three of us," Oki muttered.

"Three?" Ratchet said. "I count six!" The large raccoon stepped aside, and there were Professor Bumblebean, Captain Jinx, and Uncle Griffinskitch, all covered head to foot in dust and grime.

"You're alive!" Kendra cried, running forward to hug her ragged uncle.

"Why . . . yes," the old wizard muttered, uncomfortably returning her hug.

"We were returned to our natural states when you opened the box," Professor Bumblebean explained.

"It was you who saved us when the room came crashing down," Kendra said to her uncle.

"Humph," Uncle Griffinskitch muttered. "Yes, luckily my staff started working just in time to put you and Oki under that cauldron."

"But where did you come from, Ratchet?" Kendra asked.

"I was waiting outside that darn riddle door for you folks to come back," Ratchet explained. "But then the castle started to shake and rumble. Soon, there were all sorts of cracks and holes in the walls, and I found my way into the vault. As soon as this bell started ringing, I knew I was close to you."

"But how did you get past all the monsters?" Oki asked. "And through the swamp?"

"Yeesh," Ratchet said, rolling his eyes, "I am a world-class inventor, you know."

Kendra looked about the remains of the vault. The walls had caved in, and bright warm sunshine was spilling onto the scarred and battled-damaged floor.

"Most of the castle seems to have collapsed since you opened the box," Jinx said to Kendra.

"I'm sorry about opening it," Kendra said. "But I just couldn't see any other way. . ."

"It's okay, Kendra," Uncle Griffinskitch said. "You were able to do what the rest of us could not. You were able to confront your secret."

"But I helped an Unger!" Kendra said desperately. "I committed the worst crime known to Een!"

"We know," Professor Bumblebean said. "Even though we were stone, we heard everything that passed between you and the dragon."

"But—," Kendra began.

"Enough!" Uncle Griffinskitch snorted. "Listen, Kendra, you were brave, braver than any Een I've ever known. So be brave yet. Everything will be okay. I promise, there will be time enough to discuss the Unger later. First, we must get off this mountain."

"Your uncle's right," Jinx said. "Now that the dragon is dead, every Unger, Goojun, and giant from here to Een will be swarming over these rocks to scavenge for treasure."

She had no sooner spoken than they suddenly heard a

very loud "tee hee." They all turned to see Pugglemud on the other side of the rubble. He had somehow escaped from his prison and was now swimming amidst the rocks and remains of Rumor's treasure.

"Gold, gold, beautiful gold!" he sang. "The most wondrous thing I ever know'd!"

"Listen up, fool!" Jinx shouted. "Monsters are headed this way! You'd better come with us, unless you want to end up in some Goojun's stew pot!"

But Pugglemud seemed oblivious to them.

"Leave him," Uncle Griffinskitch said. "He's picked his fate, and there's nothing we can do to help him."

"Wait a minute!" Kendra said. "Where did Oki go?"

"I'm here," Oki replied, appearing from behind a large rock. "Look what I found: the Box of Whispers."

Uncle Griffinskitch hobbled over to look at the now-empty chest.

"What's going to happen, Uncle Griffinskitch?" Kendra asked. "Will the magic curtain fail now that the whispers have all escaped?"

"No," the old wizard said, stroking his long white beard. "Not unless someone discovers its secret and decides to undo the curtain. But who knows where the secret of the curtain has gone? It may never be found. The whispers have scattered across the wide world."

Kendra picked up the box and examined it. It didn't pulse or radiate; it felt and looked just like any other normal box.

"Uh, Elder Griffinskitch," Ratchet said, "there's just one more thing."

"Humph," Uncle Griffinskitch muttered, turning to the raccoon. "And what's that, Ringtail?"

"It's about this darn bell," Ratchet said. "Can you turn it off? It's driving me crazy!"

CHAPTER 26

Kendra and the Council

In later years, Kendra could never clearly remember the journey home. It was all a blur, filled with hazy memories that moved about her mind like a dream. Her faulty recollections were mostly due to illness, for only a day after leaving the mountains, Kendra came down with a raging fever. What caused it, no one could say, but she had been fighting her secret for so long that she herself supposed that everything had just caught up with her. Whatever the case, her condition deteriorated so rapidly that she soon couldn't even walk, and her uncle and friends had to carry her on a makeshift stretcher.

What she did remember of the journey was mostly just smatterings of conversation that she overheard as she tossed and turned in her delirium.

"What will you do, Elder Griffinskitch?" she heard Professor Bumblebean ask her uncle one night. "Will you tell the other elders that Kendra helped the Unger? They may well wish to expel her."

"You know, we could keep it a secret," Ratchet declared. "Myself, I'll never tell, I swear."

"Humph," Uncle Griffinskitch muttered. "No more secrets. Have we not learned anything from all of this? We will tell the truth."

And that's the last Kendra remembered hearing. Uncle Griffinskitch might be on her side, but it seemed that she would be left to face an uncertain fate. She slipped further into the delirium of her illness.

The next thing Kendra knew, she was back home, in her own bed. She wasn't sure how she got there, though she had a vague recollection of Ratchet carrying her through the curtain, holding her as they traveled down the River Wink (Jinx must have steered the boat), and bringing her to the house. When she opened her eyes, the raccoon was still there, sitting at her bedside.

"Well, it seems your fever's finally broken," Ratchet said. "Soon you'll be strong enough to take on the world again!"

Kendra smiled weakly. "Where's Uncle Griffinskitch?" she asked.

"Oh, he'll be back soon, not to worry," Ratchet said, holding her hand. "He's just off talking to those elders. Lots to talk about now, you can imagine. With all the secrets released, there's quite the hullabaloo across Een."

"Everyone must be angry at me for releasing their secrets," Kendra murmured.

"Oh, no, not really," Ratchet said. "Most of the secrets weren't all that serious, you know. Mostly stuff like so-and-so stealing another so-and-so's recipe for twinkleberry pie. In a way, I think most of us are glad that the whispers were set free. It's cleared the air, quite frankly."

"What about the elders?" Kendra asked.

"What about them?" Ratchet asked.

"They want to banish me," Kendra stated, as if she were sure of the fact.

"No, no," Ratchet said quickly. "No decision's been made yet. Don't go worrying about anything except getting some rest and eating your soup. Old Griffinskitch made you a whole pot."

So Kendra did what the raccoon said and spent the next few days recovering her strength. Ratchet rarely left her side. Uncle Griffinskitch came in and out. He was kind to Kendra, more so than he had ever been, but she couldn't help noticing how worried he looked. Part of her wanted to ask him about his meetings with the elders, but part of her was afraid. So she let it lie. There would be time enough to face it when she was stronger.

She had other visitors too during this time, including Professor Bumblebean and even Captain Jinx. Oki had to sneak over to the house, for his mother was convinced that Kendra was contagious and didn't want her son contracting some "horrible dragon disease."

Then one morning, as Kendra was gobbling down her breakfast (she was strong enough now to get out of bed), Uncle Griffinskitch announced: "Today we must go before the elders."

A shiver went down Kendra's back. "Must we?" she asked timidly.

"Humph," her uncle grunted. "I'm afraid so, Kendra. But I will be there with you. We'll face them together."

Kendra nodded, but she stared into the bottom of her cereal bowl, unable to look up at him.

She tugged her braids (or what was left of them, for they were still growing back after being burnt by the dragon) all the way to the Elder Stone. When they arrived, the rest of the company was awaiting them: Oki, Jinx, Professor Bumblebean, and even Ratchet. Together they went into the council chambers and stood before the elders.

"I see our young champion has recovered her strength at last," Winter Woodsong said, looking directly at Kendra.

"Aye," Uncle Griffinskitch uttered when Kendra didn't reply. In truth, she was too nervous to speak.

"It seems the orb chose well, young Kandlestar," Winter told the girl.

"Ma'am?" Kendra asked.

"Why, you defeated the Red Thief," Winter said. "Quite an achievement for an eleven-year-old, don't you think?"

"Ah, but no normal eleven-year-old," Elder Nora Neverfar said with a smile.

"Indeed," Winter agreed, "she possesses the qualities that many of us do not. Now I see why the orb chose her. She was able to face the truth. Her truth."

"But now the whispers have been released," Kendra said, trembling before the old woman. "The secret of the curtain has been lost."

"Perhaps we were foolish to lock our secrets in a box, trying to ignore them," Winter said. "For countless years we have hidden behind the curtain, but if we mean to reclaim its secret, we'll have to go into the world and search for it."

"I'm going to find my family out there," Kendra suddenly declared. She didn't even know what made her say it. But she knew it was true. Through all the days of her recuperation, it was the one thought that had given her the strength to get better, to get past whatever fate the Council of Elders was going to decide for her.

Winter looked at her with a start.

"Maybe not today or even tomorrow, but one day I will," Kendra said. She could feel her spark again inside of her. She was starting to get used to it.

"I, for one, believe she will find them," Elder Enid Evermoon said, leaning forward and looking intently at Kendra. "She's got a wee bit of her mother in her, wouldn't you say? In my opinion, that means she can do anything, if she sets her mind to it."

"Is that so?" Elder Burdock Brown growled, his one eyebrow knotting angrily on his forehead. "You may be right. After all, she will have plenty of time to look once we banish her from Een!"

"You can't banish her!" Ratchet cried, shaking his fist.

"Easy, Mr. Ringtail," Winter said, turning to cast a critical eye at Burdock. "Elder Burdock does not speak for the council alone. No decision has been made yet about Kendra's fate."

"Kendra," Skarab Strom said, leaning forward. "Do you have anything to say in your defense?"

"What do you mean?" she asked.

"Why did you help the beast?" Burdock demanded.

"He would have died without my help," Kendra said.

"Good!" Burdock snarled. "It would have been just one less Unger!"

"You weren't there!" Kendra said hotly. "You didn't look into his eyes and see how scared he was."

"Then you're not sorry for your actions?" Burdock asked.

Kendra stared hard at the angry old elder. "No," she admitted in a firm voice.

At once, the elders broke into heated debate.

"Not sorry!"

"An Unger!"

"Should there be any further discussion?" Burdock demanded, his voice reigning over the others. "The girl helped

an Unger, and she doesn't even repent for her mistake. Cast her through the curtain, I say. Let's be done with her!"

"Now wait a minute!" Uncle Griffinskitch cried, hobbling over to stand between Kendra and the elders. Up until that moment, he had been hanging back, and Kendra had worried that he wouldn't speak in her defense because he was ashamed, too. "Did my niece not save all of Een? Will you praise her one action, only to punish her for the other?"

"According to Een laws, she did indeed commit a grave crime," Elder Skarab Strom said.

"Humph!" Uncle Griffinskitch muttered. "You heard her. You weren't there. None of us were. Who's to say what any of us would have done in the same situation?"

"So you condone her helping the Unger?" Burdock demanded. "Pity, Gregor. You should be ashamed of her."

"Ashamed?" Uncle Griffinskitch exclaimed in his deep, booming voice. "I am ashamed of many things in my life, but my niece is not one of them. Indeed, if anything, I . . . I . . . I am proud of Kendra!"

Burdock gasped.

"You heard me right!" the old wizard said, shaking angrily. "Proud. Because Kendra has shown the ability to think for herself, not of herself. She helped the Unger because she felt it was the right thing to do."

"This is nonsense!" Burdock shouted. "I demand that Kendra Kandlestar be expelled!"

"If Kendra goes, then so do I," Uncle Griffinskitch proclaimed loudly.

"Me too," Ratchet said, stepping forward.

"And me," Oki said in the bravest voice Kendra had ever heard from him.

"I won't leave her," Jinx said.

"My word, neither will I!" Professor Bumblebean declared, joining his companions by stepping forth.

"Fools!" Burdock growled venomously. "How can you talk such nonsense?"

"With all due respect, Elder Burdock," Professor Bumblebean said, "you simply have not been through the adventures that we have experienced. I think I speak for us all when I say we shall stand together. If one goes, all go."

"Well put, Professor," Uncle Griffinskitch said.

"Then banish them all!" Burdock sneered. "Such fools should keep good company!"

Once again, the elders broke into argument, until at last Winter raised her hand to silence them.

"We will vote on this matter, for this is the way of Eens,"

Winter declared. "Elders, make your choice. Shall we cast Kendra Kandlestar from Een?"

Kendra couldn't bear to watch. With a gulp, she closed her eyes. A thousand thoughts raced through her mind. If she were banished, would Uncle Griffinskitch and the rest of the company really come with her? Where would they live? How would they survive? Then she felt the tiny paw of Oki shaking her excitedly, and Kendra opened her eyes. The council sat gravely before her, but only Burdock and Skarab Strom had raised their hands.

"The council has spoken," Winter announced. "Kendra, you shall stay in the land of Een. Indeed, may you go forth a hero!"

"A hero?" Burdock huffed.

"Indeed," Winter declared, and with these words she dismissed the council.

The chamber emptied, and soon only Kendra and Uncle Griffinskitch remained.

"Did you really mean what you said?" Kendra asked the old wizard. "Are you really proud of me?"

"Well . . . I, that is to say . . . yes," her uncle replied. "More than you can ever know, Kendra."

She could no longer hold back her tears. Kendra threw

her arms around the old Een and buried her head in his long white beard. She hugged him so tightly that he wheezed for air.

"And about your family," Uncle Griffinskitch said after she released him. "I would be honored, Kendra, if you would let me look for them with you."

"We'll do it together," she said happily.

"Humph," Uncle Griffinskitch murmured, and it was an odd sort of humph, the type Kendra had never heard from her uncle. As far as humphs go, she realized, it was altogether happy.

The End

Author's Note and Acknowledgements

"Of all base passions, fear is the most accurs'd."
— William Shakespeare, Henry VI, Part I

This story, of course, is in many ways about fear or, perhaps more accurately said, about confronting fear. Like our young Kendra, we find that we must face many fears throughout our lives, and we embark on many journeys, each fraught with its own set of perils. I think writing a story is like going on a journey. It has incredible highs and lows. Sometimes you feel elated. Sometimes you feel exhausted. And many times, you need the help of those around you.

Thankfully, on this journey, I had the support of many friends, colleagues, and mentors, who picked me up, dusted me off, and set me on my way when the going got tough. To recognize everyone would be a difficult task indeed, but I take these few lines now to do my best.

Firstly, thank you, Gabriella, my steadfast companion on this journey. You were my Jinx, Oki, Griffinskitch, and Professor all, and each footfall along the path would have been tremendously difficult (and not half as fun!) if not for your constant support, encouragement, and sacrifice.

To my family—Dad, Mom, Gus, Ute—I appreciate that each of you rolled up your sleeves to help make *Whispers* a success, from spreading the news about the book to helping build a truly fantastic model of my fabled box. But especially, I thank you, Crystal—little sister, lover of literature, beloved fellow nerd. I cannot imagine going through the process of writing a book without having access to your passion and unbridled zeal.

My sincere gratitude to Mike. Your humble and constant friendship (not to mention your ability to crunch numbers and make sense of the business side of selling books) was invaluable to me.

I give special recognition to fellow author Diana Guerrero; you not only lent me your marketing savvy, but—more importantly—a comfortable shoulder when the going got tough.

My heartfelt thanks to my friends Renuka, Caroline, Derill, Diana, Annie, Stephanie, Linda, Joon, and to all my students; you never failed to lift me with your enthusiasm and energy.

Of course, I must thank the expert publishing team at Brown Books—Milli, Kathryn, Cindy, Brian, Deanne and Erica: you actually made the *process* of publishing a thrilling and exciting one. I would be remiss, too, not to mention my editors; firstly, Darlene Hughes: you helped me early on in the genesis of *Whispers* and gave me the royal kick in the bottom I needed to make the story what it is today; and secondly to Liza Burby: you helped guide little Kendra home on the last leg of her journey with your expert advice and knowledge.

Finally, to Dōv: where would I be, if not for you? You taught me to look into the dimly-lit corners. I could never thank you enough, my kind mentor, gifted sage, stern teacher, master opener of boxes.

Lee Edward Födi has been writing and illustrating stories about magic, monsters, and meddlesome animals for as long as he can remember. Growing up on a farm, he harbored childhood aspirations of taking over the family business. Unfortunately, this dream came to an abrupt end when he accidentally ran the tractor over his dad's outhouse (thankfully, his dad was not inside at the time). As a result, Födi went on to pursue his love of art, mythology, and storytelling, all of which (luckily) do not require any skill in operating heavy machinery. Födi currently lives and works in Vancouver, Canada.

Find out more at www.leefodi.com.